ANGELA BRITNELL

◆

FEELING
FESTIVE

Complete and Unabridged

LINFORD
ROMANCE

LINFORD
Leicester

First published in Great Britain in 2019

First Linford Edition
published 2021

A catalogue record for this book is available
from the British Library.

ISBN 978–1–4448–4804–5

Published by
Ulverscroft Limited
Anstey, Leicestershire

Printed and bound in Great Britain by
TJ Books Ltd., Padstow, Cornwall

This book is printed on acid-free paper

Twelve Days to Go

Mollie's top lip wobbled.

'You said we could do anything I wanted.'

Before this developed into a full-blown on-the-verge-of-Christmas meltdown Rachel had to come up with an appealing alternative. Fast. Any minute now her niece's huge blue eyes would brim over with tears and there'd be no coming back.

'I meant it, sweetheart, but I've got a better idea.'

'Better than going to Holly Jolly Christmas Land?' Suspicion oozed from every pore in the little girl's body.

Rachel's prized crown as Number One Fun Aunt would pass to Anna's moody sister if she wasn't careful, but the mini-theme park would be a nightmare where she was concerned, full of over-excited manic children and painful family memories.

'Absolutely.' Ideas raced around her

brain and she methodically kicked each out in turn.

She'd promised they could do anything her niece wanted between now and Christmas to escape from the hospital without a tantrum. Mollie had clung on to her mother and pleaded with Anna to let her stay.

'I'll curl up really small and no-one will know I'm here. I can talk to the babies and tell them all about Daddy.'

That even brought tears to Rachel's eyes and Harry, her tough soldier brother now serving in Afghanistan, often teased that she was harder than most of the men in his unit.

His joking words came with a sad half-smile because he knew only too well what sucked the softness out of her.

'Well?' Mollie gave her blonde ponytail a dismissive toss.

'You've heard the carol about the twelve days of Christmas? We've got twelve days until . . . '

'Mummy has our babies and Daddy comes home.' Mollie bounced on her heels.

It might not prove that simple but she couldn't burst her niece's happy bubble. Rachel's sister-in-law Anna was pregnant with twins and over the last month her blood pressure had steadily increased to the point where the doctors were concerned about possible pre-eclampsia.

In an effort to prevent her going into early labour they'd insisted she be hospitalised on strict bed rest where they could keep her under observation. Last week Anna had phoned Rachel, sounding frantic.

'My parents aren't up to coping with Mollie for longer than a night or two. I could send her to my sister in Leeds but that would mean missing all the end of term activities at school and I can't do that to her on top of everything else.

'Is there any chance the corporate world can do without you for a few weeks?'

Rachel had perfected the role of doting aunt. She flew in from Paris, Dubai or Rome loaded down with presents, disrupted her niece's routine in a good way and then left again before boredom set in on either side.

But coping with the school run, providing regular meals and dealing with the endless curiosity of a smart six-year-old was completely different.

'I can count the big red crosses on the calendar,' Mollie boasted.

'Good. That will help with our plan.'

'What plan? And why can't we go to Holly Jolly Christmas Land?'

Rachel clenched her jaw and struggled to smile.

'Because that's something you do in one day and it's over with but my idea will be fun for twelve whole days. Doesn't that sound awesome?'

'Maybe.'

Persuading multi-million pound companies to invest in computer security software was easier than talking one small child out of something she'd set her heart on.

'This way you get to pick twelve things instead of only one.'

'Anything I want?'

She'd been caught out with 'anything' before. Time to sneak in a few caveats.

'Remember you've got school for three more days and we can't go too far from home.'

'Mummy makes a list. Do you know how to make a list?' Mollie rattled on. 'I can write my name and stuff but lists are hard.' She ran to the kitchen and yanked out a drawer. 'Here.' A pad of paper ended up in Rachel's hand.

'First we need a Christmas tree.' Her smile faltered. 'Daddy always picks out the best one and cuts it down with a sharp knife thing.'

Obviously Rachel's plan to buy a pre-lit, pre-decorated tree in a box from the nearest shop wouldn't work.

'I'm sure we can manage.' Rachel started the list. 'What else?'

'Christmas biscuits. Mummy makes Father Christmas ones and snowmen and angels. They have icing and sprinkles and glitter. Lots of glitter.'

'Sounds yummy.'

By Mollie's dubious expression the little girl must have overheard her parents laughing about Rachel's non-existent baking skills.

'Daddy promised to take me ice-skating this year now I'm big.' Her little face crumpled.

Finally an easy thing for Rachel to handle.

'It's not a problem. I taught your daddy to skate so I'm sure I can teach you.'

'Why didn't his mummy or daddy show him?'

Rachel couldn't speak. Raking up the past hurt.

'I said . . .'

'I heard you, sweetie.' She crouched down in front of her niece. 'They didn't know how to skate but I did. What else is going on our twelve days of Christmas list?'

'Hot chocolate before bed. Every night.' Mollie wagged her finger. 'Mummy makes it with real chocolate and it must have marshmallows.'

6

'We haven't got any chocolate or marshmallows.'

'Ask Mr Roy.'

'Who's Mr Roy?'

'The man who lives there.' Mollie grabbed Rachel's hand and dragged her over to the living-room window. 'With the pretty lights.'

She pointed enviously to the house next door. The garish Christmas decorations included Father Christmas with his sleigh on the roof and inflatable snowmen and penguins dotted around the front garden.

'Put lights on my list, please. Lots of them.'

'OK.' Agreeing didn't mean a competition. 'But we'll have to go food shopping ourselves. We can't ask him for chocolate and marshmallows.'

'Why not? Mummy does and Mr Roy borrows Daddy's tools.'

Rachel had got out of the habit of village life where neighbours helped each other out.

'All right, but just this one time.'

Her niece beamed. Plainly she'd got her aunt exactly where she wanted.

Outside the front door, decked with a wreath made of grinning Father Christmas faces and with a massive red bow, Rachel cringed as she rang the bell.

'Hark! The Herald Angels Sing' jangled merrily in the clear night air.

'Isn't it fun? Can we . . .'

'No, sweetheart.' Anna would never forgive her if she returned home to a carol-playing doorbell.

'Wow! I needed an angel to stick on the top of my tree. Are you here to apply for the job?' The tall, handsome man filled the doorway and flashed a white-toothed grin at Mollie.

'Don't be silly, Mr Roy, it's me. Mollie.'

For the first time since Rachel arrived she heard her niece's unrestrained laughter and silently thanked the man for performing a miracle.

She didn't realise she was staring until he winked and made her blush. His bright green eyes twinkled. No man should look drop-dead gorgeous wearing a hideous scarlet jumper with a fuzzy green Christmas tree and bouncing gold baubles stretched across his broad chest, but he managed it.

'Of course you are. Silly old me.' He playfully smacked his head. 'And who's this lovely lady you've brought to see me?'

'I'm Rachel Trewarren. Harry's sister.'

'We need chocolate and marshmallows soooo badly, Mr Roy,' Mollie piped up.

'That's not how we ask for something, is it?' Rachel corrected her.

'It's OK. We're old friends, aren't we, kiddo?'

She vaguely remembered Anna mentioning an American who lived nearby. Did that explain the man's Christmas obsession?

'Let me guess.' He crouched down. 'Hot chocolate?' At her nod he lowered his voice to a stage whisper. 'Does your aunt know how to fix it right?'

'How difficult can it be?'

The question earned her an amused smile.

'Y'all talking about it made me fancy hot chocolate, too. How about I fix us all some?'

'Oh, yes, yes, yes!' Mollie jumped up and down. 'Please, Aunty Rach. Mr Roy makes the best hot chocolate in the whole world.' Her cheeks coloured. 'Don't tell Mummy.'

'I don't think we . . .'

'Sorry, I forgot to introduce myself properly.' He sprang up and stuck out his hand leaving her no choice but to take hold of it.

Large. Warm. Strong. All the things a man's hand should be.

'Mollie finds Roy easier to say but it's Royce. Royce Carver. Native of Nashville, Tennessee, and temporary resident of St Kellow. I'm . . . between jobs at the moment.'

'And in the meantime you keep the Christmas light industry in business.'

He gave her a quizzical look.

'Oh, heavens, you're one of those.' His rich warm voice resonated with amusement.

'One of what?'

'A grouch. Grinch. Scrooge. Choose any that apply.' Royce's sad head-shake almost drew a smile out of her.

'Just because I dislike hearing carols played for months on end in every shop and prefer tasteful white lights to . . .' She trailed off as she realised her opinions might sound like criticism.

'We're gonna have to work on your aunt,' he assured Mollie. 'Let's start with real hot chocolate and go from there.'

'Mr Roy can help with our list.'

'We'll see.'

'In you come.' Royce ushered them through the door.

'If you're good, Mr Roy gives you extra marshmallows.' Mollie imparted the information very seriously.

Royce leaned in closer and a teasing hint of his clean, masculine cologne teased her nose.

'If you're bad you get extra, extra marshmallows.' Her attempt at a disapproving frown didn't fool him, judging by the hint of mischief tugging at his mouth.

In his warm, cluttered, spice-scented kitchen, fresh gingerbread biscuits cooled on a wire rack, begging to be eaten. Unsurprisingly, the ceiling was draped in red crepe paper garlands and flashing green lights and a trio of fat china Father Christmases perched on top of the refrigerator.

Rachel watched silently as Royce grated chocolate, heated a pan of milk and stirred in the pile of chocolate before adding several heaped spoonfuls of sugar and a sprinkling of warm spices.

He did all this while telling Mollie lame knock-knock jokes to a background of Christmas carols playing on the radio. Royce shared out the hot drink into three mugs and grabbed several bags of marshmallows from the cupboard.

'Big or small? Pink or white?'

Mollie stuck her tongue in the corner of her mouth while she thought, reminding Rachel of her brother.

'Some of each?' Plainly she didn't expect her hopeful request to succeed but Royce gave an approving nod and topped each mug with a mound of marshmallows.

'Tell me about the list.' Royce hunched over his hot chocolate and concentrated on listening to Mollie's garbled explanation. 'Wow, that's such a cool idea. You're a lucky little girl. Your aunt is one smart cookie.'

'She's not a cookie, she's an aunt.'

'I sure am dumb today.' With an assessing sweep of his startling green eyes he studied her from head to toe.

'Yep, you're right. Definitely an aunt.' Her face flamed. 'Mollie, while your hot drink cools down a bit would you like to check out my new dancing reindeer in the other room?'

Royce gave Rachel a conspiratorial wink.

'You can see them, too, in a minute. I don't want you to feel left out.'

When Mollie disappeared so did his smile.

'Catch me up with how Anna's doing and when Harry might make it home.

Poor guy. I know he's torn up worrying about them.'

Something about his quiet kindness made Rachel tell him about today's scene at the hospital.

'I'm hopeless at this.'

'What?'

'The stand-in parent thing.'

'Don't beat yourself up. It's clear you love her and you're trying your best. That's all she needs.'

'Maybe.' Rachel wasn't convinced. 'Were your parents nuts about Christmas, too?'

'My parents? Hardly. My folks refused to 'waste' money on anything connected to a holiday they didn't believe in. No tree. No decorations. No presents.' Royce shrugged.

'A therapist told me I'm overcompensating now. I thought about what she said and decided I'm not harming myself or anyone else so I'm not keen to be 'cured'.'

Mollie raced back in.

'They're totally awesome, Aunt Rach.

14

They sing the Rudolph song.'

They would.

'Drink your hot chocolate and then we'll leave . . . Mr Roy in peace.' She caught the edge of Royce's disappointment as Mollie's shoulders drooped and her mouth settled into a pout. Any minute now a tantrum would erupt.

The List Goes On . . .

'Where's your list, Mollie?' Royce asked quickly.

'We left it . . .'

'You left it.' Mollie dug out a scrunched up piece of paper and thrust it at him.

Royce sensed this was more important to the little girl than simply Christmas treats. Anna and Harry were great neighbours who welcomed him when others weren't sure how to treat a lone American who suddenly appeared, took a long term let on a house and didn't appear to do anything.

If Mollie needed something positive to get through the next few days he'd do his utmost to help even if meant doing battle with Rachel's obvious reticence.

Usually he was drawn to petite, curvy blondes with a bubbly personality but the self-contained, willowy beauty with her very French black clothes and wary grey eyes ticked none of those boxes yet still stirred his interest.

16

'For a start the list must be on proper Christmassy paper or it won't be official.' He grabbed a snowman pen and a pad of paper decorated with robins and holly.

Rachel couldn't help rolling her eyes.

He ignored her and carefully wrote down Mollie's wishes.

1. Find and cut down the best real Christmas tree and decorate it.
2. Bake Christmas biscuits.
3. Go ice skating.
4. Make hot chocolate with marshmallows every night.
5. Hang up Christmas lights inside and outside the house.
6. Buy a red party dress and sparkly shoes to wear on Christmas Day.
7. Go carol singing.
8. See Father Christmas and pet one of his reindeer.

Rachel's frown deepened.

Royce took a guess she probably spent December 25th pretending it was a regular day if she was forced to take the time off work.

'Twelve things is a lot, Mr Roy,' Mollie complained, 'and I'm not allowed to put Holly Jolly Christmas Land on the list but it's what I want the mostest.'

'Why . . .'

'We've already discussed that, Mollie.' Rachel's curt response made the little girl's eyes fill with tears. Royce didn't admit he'd be going to the seasonal theme park next week with a group of at-risk children that he helped to mentor.

'You can think some more about it, kiddo. You've got enough to start on.'

'That's a brilliant idea,' Rachel chimed in.

'Thank you, ma'am.'

'Ma'am? I'm not the Queen.'

'Thank heavens for that! You'd probably lock me up in the Tower of London . . . or worse.' He waggled his eyebrows and Mollie dissolved into fits of giggles while Rachel remained stony faced.

'We really must go now.' Rachel stood

18

up. 'Thank you for the hot chocolate and for your help with the list.'

'Don't forget to take it with you.' He passed the paper over and a shot of electricity tingled through his skin as their fingers brushed. 'Any help you need, you come right on over.' Royce grasped her hand before she could pull it away. 'I mean it. Anything.'

'That's very kind of you.'

They both knew she hadn't come by choice but Mollie and proximity were on his side. He would bide his time.

★ ★ ★

After the quickest bath on record Rachel ignored her niece's protests and tucked her into bed.

'You've got school in the morning.'

'We've must get our tree tomorrow.' Mollie's eyes popped back open and she jerked up in the bed. 'Daddy says you have to be quick before everyone gets the best ones.'

Rachel gritted her teeth.

'We need to ask Daddy where to buy one. Mummy and I talk to him on the computer.'

'I'm sorry, sweetheart, but we can't right now.' She explained that Harry was busy working. Her brother had warned Anna he'd be out of touch for a while and couldn't say exactly when he'd be back at the base. Living with that level of uncertainty would drive Rachel crazy and gave her an increased respect for her sister-in-law.

'Mr Roy will know. He knows everything.'

No way was she begging their neighbour for any more help unless it was a dire emergency and a Christmas tree didn't count, in her book. Royce Carver unsettled her. His perceptive eyes saw too much and his alluring southern drawl reminded her of butter melting on hot crumpets.

'I'll track down a Christmas tree farm tomorrow and we'll go after school.'

'Promise?'

'I promise.'

'Cross your heart?' Mollie's fierceness amused her.

'Yes.'

'Good. It's story time now.'

'Just one.'

'I want the 'Jolly Christmas Postman'.'

Trust Mollie. Last time one of the envelopes ripped after she tried to rush through the long, fiddly book. Rachel perched on the bed and Mollie snuggled into her, smelling of strawberry soap.

For a fleeting moment Rachel envied Anna and Harry before brushing away the thought. She had a good life. A challenging job. An elegant apartment in the centre of Paris. A varied social life with plenty of opportunities to travel. There was nothing to complain about. Family life was fine in small doses but she'd be itching to get away when her duties were over.

'Come on, Aunty Rach.'

She did as she was told and started to read. There was no opportunity for introspection around small children.

Royce left the lights off when he took his glass of whisky in the living-room. While he sat in the dark and cradled the glass in his hands he wondered about Rachel. The last thing he wanted was her sympathy. He never told people about his lousy childhood so why her? Because her grey eyes didn't leave him room to lie. Of course, he hadn't told her the full truth.

He'd never forget his embarrassment when his parents challenged the second grade teacher who told him off for reducing several of his classmates to tears. Royce had casually repeated what he'd been brought up to believe — that Santa Claus didn't exist and Christmas was simply a money-making scheme dreamed up to fleece poor people.

Royce wasn't naive and the fact that many people in the world didn't know where their next meal would come from didn't escape him.

He understood some of the Christmas excesses were — well, excessive, but wasn't the general air of goodwill a positive thing? And what about sweet little Mollie today? The kid had a lot on her plate and if a herd of dancing toy reindeer made her laugh was that so terrible?

What had made Rachel and Harry so different? Harry echoed Royce's own philosophy of life and tried to find the humour in any given situation. Royce didn't doubt his friend was totally serious when it came to his job but in his own laid-back way. But Rachel? A few times her implacable mouth softened at the edges until she reined in a smile at the last second.

This wasn't getting him anywhere. He ambled into the kitchen to pop a couple of mince pies in the oven. While they warmed up he'd check on his outside lights.

'Making sure you're still using more than your fair share of the country's electricity?'

He spotted Rachel over the hedge separating their gardens.

'I'm paying for it. What's your problem

anyway?'The silence should have pleased him but her distraught face in the flickering coloured lights made him feel a complete heel. 'Forget it. You've had a tough day. We'll start fresh tomorrow.'

'Start what?'

'Rachel. Please. You've got it all wrong.' Royce kept his voice measured and calm. 'Anna and Harry are my best friends here and I'm not gonna mess that up by making any unwanted moves on you. I'd better go.'

'I've got mince pies in the oven and they'll burn.' He heard her snigger. 'You should have been around in Cromwell's time — you'd have made a great Puritan. Good night, Scrooge.'

He marched inside and slammed the door. Tomorrow he'd apologise but right now Royce wasn't convinced that goodwill to all men included sarcastic women.

She'd Show Mr Christmas!

Rachel had forgotten that Cornish winters were habitually mild and damp and the prospect of tramping around Christmas tree farms in persistent drizzle didn't improve her dire mood. After she picked up Mollie from school they'd go to Sugar Tree Farm. It had the best online reviews and the largest selection plus her niece would love that the staff were all dressed as elves and handed out free candy canes.

Scrooge? How dare he? She'd prove to Mr Royce Carver that she could do Christmas as well as anyone.

Rachel slammed Harry's battered old Land Rover into gear and headed back to St Kellow. As she approached the tiny village, about five miles from the coast, she slowed down. Through the clearing clouds she spotted the church spire.

When she was growing up and they'd been out for the day Mum called this view the signal that they were home and always told their dad to take his time driving down Potter's Lane.

When Harry told her at Easter they'd decided to settle in Cornwall after he left the army next year and had already bought a house in St Kellow, Rachel thought he was mad. Now she began to understand.

Two hours later Rachel collapsed in the nearest chair and gazed around the room. Who knew it would take so long to put up a few decorations? Mollie wanted them to do the tree and lights together but she'd raided every Christmas shop in St Mervyn for additional decorations.

She'd struggled to see things through the eyes of a six-year-old. The result was an oversized wreath on the front door decorated with flashing lights and a tacky gold bow, a row of dancing snowmen across the mantel and dramatic swags of red velvet ribbon all the way up the banister rail.

She'd reserved the best surprise for Mollie's room and set up a miniature tree. Everything was in her niece's favourite colour, from the garish bright pink lights to the sparkling pink fairy.

She tightened the belt on her black raincoat and pulled up the hood before venturing back out. If she ran she'd just about make it to school on time. How would Anna manage this with twin babies in tow?

'Careful, I almost knocked you over.'

Royce's firm hands grasped her shoulders and kept her upright. She'd been too busy barrelling along the path to notice him walking in the other direction.

'I've come to apologise.'

'I don't have time to listen right now.'

'Make time — please.' Royce's deep, warm voice got to her again.

'I really can't. I've got . . . ten minutes and counting to make it to the school gates.'

'You got any problem with me walking along, too?'

'I suppose not.' At least his heavy black raincoat mostly concealed whatever ugly jumper he'd chosen today and only a flash of something white and shiny showed around the neck.

'It's a mohair snowman, if you're interested.'

'Where on earth do you find them?'

'Online, mostly.' Royce pulled open his coat to show off the snowman with flashing eyes and buttons and a sticking out fake carrot nose made of orange felt. 'They do this design in women's sizes, too.'

'Fascinating.'

'Maybe Santa will put one in your stocking.'

'He'd better not.' The warning made him smile. Royce's smile didn't simply involve his mouth and twinkling eyes but etched tantalising creases in his whole face. Sure signs of someone for whom smiling was a regular occurrence.

'I really am sorry. Don't know what got into me last night.'

'I did,' Rachel confessed. 'I stirred you up for no reason other than . . . perverseness.' Hordes of noisy children spilled out of the school and into the road. 'I'm sorry, too, but I honestly don't have time for . . . anything.' She watched the message sink home.

'Oh, Aunty Rach, you asked Mr Roy to go tree shopping with us. You're the best. Thank you.' Mollie flung her arms around Rachel and over her head Royce gave her a questioning look.

'Mr Roy isn't coming to the Christmas tree farm. He was just out for a walk and came this far with me.' The lie made her face burn but she couldn't back down now. He'd be happy to help out but next it would be the lights and whatever else Mollie dreamed up. Taking care of her niece was her job.

'Let's go. You need to change out of your uniform.' Mollie's jaw jutted out and she sensed a mutinous refusal coming on. 'You want a tree, don't you?'

'I'm real sorry, kiddo, but I've got other plans now. Maybe you can invite me over to see your tree later?'

Very underhand, Royce Carver. She plastered on an agreeable expression. Calling it a smile might stretch the truth.

'That would be lovely wouldn't it,

Mollie?'

'It'll be bigger than yours and have tons more lights won't it, Aunty Rach?'

'We'll see. We'll definitely have hot chocolate because I bought all the ingredients today.'

'Yippee.'

'Yippee indeed.' Royce echoed Mollie's excitement and gave a sly wink behind her niece's back. 'See ya later.' He shoved his hands in his pockets and strode off in the opposite direction.

'About seven o'clock,' Rachel called after him, receiving a cheerful wave in response.

★ ★ ★

That went pretty well, Royce thought. He'd unsettled Rachel again, made Mollie happy and secured an invitation to number 29. Following his instincts to Cornwall hadn't been crazy after all. His parents thought it ridiculous that he'd decided on coming to this remote spot on the basis of a favourite book that he'd been given as a boy. He'd soaked up the fascinating tales about giants, piskies, mermaids and King Arthur and promised one day he'd visit the magical land.

He hadn't come across any of the mythical creatures yet but strongly suspected Rachel of being the Cornish version of a Siren and luring him with hot chocolate.

Royce whistled 'Frosty The Snowman' as he walked towards the centre of the village. St Kellow was too far from the coast to draw many visitors.

Most people travelled to the nearby towns for work, when they could find it, because here the employment choices were limited to a small meat-packing plant and a group of artisan craft workshops based at the old primary school.

Talking to a few locals in the Harvest Moon pub one night he discovered there used to be a wide range of shops here in the days before most families owned a car.

Royce wasn't opposed to progress, far from it, but what did progress actually mean to most people? That same evening he went home and stayed up until dawn jotting down ideas for a series of magazine articles.

When he stopped writing he hadn't even been tired and contrasted that with how he felt after a day doing root canals.

He headed for Miss Mary's Tea Rooms, an old-fashioned café tucked between the post office and a Chinese takeaway. Apart from excellent tea and cakes they also sold greetings cards and sweets. In one corner of the room was a small lending library based on an honesty system that worked because Mary and her assistant, Alice, didn't miss a thing that was going on.

English brandy-soaked fruit cake was a Christmas specialty he'd fallen for big time and a large slab of that and a pot of tea would tide him over until Mollie's hot chocolate.

'You should set a good example for your patients. You're a disgrace to the dental profession,' his father had said years ago when he caught Royce dipping his hand into the bowl of free mints as they left a restaurant.

Following in his father's footsteps hadn't resulted in any level of approval — it had only given Stuart Carver more ammunition. Royce persisted for ten interminable years and built up a successful practice but a year ago he'd filled his last tooth. When he told his father about his plans it was the only time he ever saw the man lost for words.

'Write poetry for a living? Are you out of your mind, boy?'

He'd listened to his father's rant without challenging him for not listening properly. What he'd actually said was that he believed he could make a living from writing in some form whether it was journalism, short stories, novels or maybe poetry.

'We didn't spend a fortune on your undergraduate degree and four years of dental school for you to throw it in and think you're going to earn money scribbling verses no-one wants to read.'

At eighteen he didn't have the courage to stand up to his parents and gave up his dream of studying English in college. He'd had an aptitude for science but his true passion was for words.

In high school he wrote for the school newspaper, aced the poetry classes most found boring and won a prestigious, statewide short story competition. He gave all that up and concentrated on improving his grades he needed to get into Johns Hopkins University, his father's alma mater.

The only college classes he enjoyed were his required English classes and indulging his love for Whitman, Shakespeare and Wordsworth kept him going through the rest of his Biochemistry courses.

Since then he'd always written in his spare time and at thirty-five had enough confidence and money behind him to pursue his dream.

'There you go, Mr Carver.' Alice set down his tea. 'We've voted to give that one a nine out of ten.' She nodded at his snowman jumper.

'You and Mary sure are hard women to please.' Royce waved across at the older lady in charge of the till. 'What do I have to do to get a ten?'

Her blush deepened.

'Now then, sir, that'd be telling.' With a flounce she scuttled away, laughing. The first time he came in wearing a Christmas jumper, at the beginning of December, he'd startled them.

Local men didn't go in for such nonsense but they excused him on the grounds of being foreign. A Yank, of all things. Now every time he bought a new jumper he came here to show it off and give the waitresses a chance to rate it on a scale of one to ten.

He pulled out his notebook and scribbled down a few ideas for a short story.

'Your tea's gone cold,' Edith chided. 'Here's a pot of fresh hot water to top it up. My cake doesn't appreciate being ignored, either.'

'I sure am sorry. It's the best in the whole of Cornwall.'

'And how would you know?'

Royce grinned.

'Didn't I tell you I'm making a study of Cornish Christmas cakes?' He picked up the iced fruit cake and took a massive bite. 'Um. Nine out of ten, I'd say.'

'You cheeky devil.' Edith's laughter made the other customers stare.

'Better be careful. The whole village will be talking about the young Yank chatting you up.' Royce chuckled. 'Next time I'll bring a bunch of mistletoe with me and sneak a kiss.'

'You're a naughty boy. Get on with you.' With a smile she left him to his tea.

★ ★ ★

'It's crooked.' Mollie glared at the tree. 'And it's too tall. Where's the fairy going?'

Rachel almost reminded her niece she'd asked for big but maybe the top branches bent over and scraping the ceiling were a bit much.

'We could chop off a bit.'

'It will look horrible,' Mollie wailed. 'I

need my daddy.'

Now all the other decorations were forgotten, including the pink tree that earned Rachel a massive hug and kisses earlier. The Great Christmas Tree Tragedy overtook everything.

'If we cut some off the bottom it'll be fine.'

'You'll get it wrong.' Mollie snorted. 'An elf had to cut it down when we bought it.'

As soon as the tree farmer had spotted Rachel's inept efforts he plucked the sharp axe away and called one of his staff to help her out. Being rescued by a weedy teenage boy decked out in red and green and jingle bells wasn't her finest moment.

The doorbell rang. No doubt it would be Mr Christmas himself wearing his ugly jumper and bringing his own brand of festive cheer. Rachel told herself not to be childish. If he could make her niece smile again and salvage her attempt to keep up with her brother's tree-cutting skills she ought to be grateful.

'Let's look at this . . .' His mouth twitched. 'Oh my! You sure took the bigger tree thing seriously, didn't you?'

Mollie burst into giggles and Rachel struggled not to join in, but failed. Royce's eyes sparkled.

'There's nothing wrong with having a laugh,' he murmured. 'Ask your brother. Harry's got a strong sense of duty and commitment to his job but also a great sense of humour. It doesn't have to be an either/or situation.'

She shouldn't expect him to understand. No-one did, except Harry. When she didn't respond, Royce gave a quiet nod, silently telling her they'd come back to this another day.

'How did you get the tree in here on your own?'

'An elf helped Aunty Rach.' Mollie's response made him chuckle and she explained they'd needed assistance from the tree farm to get the massive thing home. She'd paid off the elf and shooed him out of the door, assuring him they'd manage just fine from there.

'We'll take it back outside and I'll cut a good ten inches or so off the bottom.'

Royce wielded an electric saw with enviable efficiency and soon had the tree stand fitted back on. Soon it stood perfectly straight in the corner of the living-room, well-watered and with the lights on.

He wiped the sheen of sweat from his forehead.

'Mind if I take off my jumper?'

'Not at all.'

'I should warn you my T-shirt . . .'

'Rudolph? Angels? Maybe a penguin?'

Royce peeled off his jumper.

'Never expected that, did you?' Rachel's cheeks burned. 'I'm a plain guy underneath all this.'

She nodded, acknowledging the crisp white T-shirt.

'I think you deserve hot chocolate for all your efforts.'

'But the tree isn't decorated yet and you'll make me go to bed soon,' Mollie protested. 'Decorating was part of today's wish. You promised.'

Rachel crouched down and held her niece's small, warm hands.

'I know. We can decorate it tonight if you don't take too long. Deal?'

'Deal.' Mollie grinned. 'But I want Mr Roy to help us.'

'I'm happy to.' He met Rachel's gaze. 'If you want?'

What could she say? His reassuring competence helped her to believe she could do this. If they got through the next couple of weeks allowing Mollie to enjoy Christmas the way a six-year-old should, with two healthy babies safely delivered and her brother back home where he belonged, that was all she wished for.

'Yes.' Her answer brought out another of his irresistible smiles.

'Are we having hot chocolate or not?' Mollie tugged her hand.

'That's a good question.' Royce winked. 'Let's see if Aunty Rach was paying attention to my master class in hot chocolate making.'

'I'll show you both,' she bragged. They didn't need to know she had practised making it three times today while Mollie was at school. She'd show Mr Christmas.

A Terrible Secret

Royce held his breath watching Rachel climb up a long ladder propped against the front wall with a string of lights draped over one shoulder. Give credit where it was due she produced some fine hot chocolate last night and they had ended up with a pretty decent tree, none the worse for the indignities it had suffered.

He stayed out of the tree decorating as much as possible because even a Christmas-phobic like Rachel could hang a few ornaments. His main contribution came in the form of lifting up Mollie high enough to place the fairy on top of the tree.

Hanging outside lights was a tricky job and for an hour he didn't move while she worked steadily away. Out of the blue Rachel suddenly yelled across at him.

'You might as well come out and watch me turn them on seeing you've been ogling at me the whole time I was up the ladder.'

'I wasn't ogling . . .'

'Call it nosing if you like — I'm not sure which is worse.'

Royce threw on a coat and hurried around to join her.

'Shall I do a drum roll?'

'Don't be daft. Just because tree cutting wasn't my thing I'm not completely incompetent.'

'I never said you were. The fact you're a Christougenniatikophobic is beside the point.'

'A what?'

'Someone with an irrational fear of Christmas.'

'I'm not a . . . whatever you called it. I simply don't like all the fuss and nonsense. If people are religious, that's different, but everyone else uses it as an excuse for . . .'

'Finding a little joy in the middle of the dreary winter season? That's terrible because we can't have people being kind and generous to each other for no good reason.'

Usually Royce defended his love of

the holidays with a smile but she set him on edge. It didn't help that he'd received a sharp e-mail from his father this morning asking when he intended to 'stop all this nonsense and get back to work.' He hadn't responded.

Rachel stared over his shoulder, the colour draining from her face.

'No. No. No.'

A man and woman in full military uniform stepped out of a large shiny black car and walked towards the gate.

'Ms Rachel Trewarren?'

'Yes.'

'I'm Major Helen Carstairs and this is Lieutenant Paul Norman from . . .'

'You can't do this to us. Harry's wife is expecting twins any day now and Little Mollie worships . . .'

'Ms Trewarren. Please.' The female officer touched Rachel's arm. 'Our news is better shared indoors.'

She frowned slightly as she glanced at Royce.

'It might be better if you left us alone, sir.'

'No.' Rachel gripped his hand. 'Please.'

'It's OK. I won't go anywhere unless you want me to.' He steered Rachel towards the house.

★ ★ ★

Ever since her headstrong brother joined the army the day after his eighteenth birthday she'd dreaded this moment. Apparently the dramatic scene where two uniformed soldiers arrive at the door bearing bad news wasn't a cliché.

'We've been to the hospital but Mrs Trewarren's doctor wouldn't allow us to speak to her because of her medical condition,' Major Carstairs explained. 'Your brother listed you as a secondary next of kin . . .'

'I know that,' Rachel snapped. 'Just tell me how he . . . died.'

'I'm not here to inform you that Major Trewarren is deceased.'

'You're not?'

'No.' The officer's voice softened. 'Two days ago Major Trewarren was on a mission and became separated from the rest of his team in the middle of a fire fight.

'He hasn't made contact since and is considered missing in action.'

'What are y'all doing to find him?' Royce jumped in. 'I appreciate you can't tell us everything but are you actively searching for him?'

Rachel knew she should be asking these questions but seemed incapable of forming a sentence.

'After our initial search of the area revealed nothing, an order from brigade headquarters put an Operation Minimise into place. That freezes all communications to and from the base until the family involved has been informed.'

Rachel's head swam.

'And now?' Royce probed.

'Now we've spoken to you that order will be lifted which means other personnel in Major Trewarren's unit can inform their families they're safe.

'A full-scale rescue operation is under way with all the resources we have at our

46

disposal.' The woman fixed them with a steady stare. 'What happens next is up to you.'

'In what way?' Rachel struggled to pull herself together for Harry's sake.

'You can choose to inform the press or keep the news among your family and close friends,' Major Carstairs explained.

'What do you recommend? We don't want anything to jeopardise Harry's safety.'

'The MOD generally advises keeping the story out of the press when there's been a possible abduction.'

'Abduction?' Royce squeezed her hand and she gained the strength to ask a terrible question. 'Would they treat him well or . . . hurt him?'

'I never lie to family members.' Carstairs's bald statement made Rachel wince. 'It could go either way.'

She would almost have preferred a white lie.

'Depending how long your brother stays missing, the MOD might decide to share the story with the press. It's bound to get out and we prefer to control the timing ourselves. At that point it would be almost impossible to hide the news from your sister-in-law and you'd have to discuss how to proceed with her medical team.'

'How do you keep us up to speed with what's happening?' Royce asked.

'You're being assigned a family liaison officer.' She passed over a business card. 'Captain Amy Worthing will be in touch later today and it's her job to help you negotiate through all this.' Carstairs gave an apologetic half-smile.

'For security reasons she can't tell you every detail but she'll release everything she's permitted to share. We can't promise your brother will return safely but we'll try our darnedest.'

'Harry is the heart of our family. Without him . . .' Rachel couldn't say any more.

The officers stood and prepared to leave.

'Ms Trewarren, we appreciate your . . .'

'Please don't say understanding because I don't understand anything right now. How can I tell Harry's six-year-old daughter that he might not be home for Christmas?' She swallowed hard. 'Not making it home at all isn't an option.'

They exchanged sympathetic glances.

'My brother isn't dead. I'd know if he was.' Rachel held her clenched fist over her heart. 'In here, and don't tell me everyone says that.' She sighed. 'I need to believe.'

'We do, too, ma'am . . . until there's concrete proof otherwise. We'll see ourselves out.'

Rachel only managed to nod. She'd lived an itinerant life for years travelling the world with her job but always with the knowledge she had Harry and his family to come home to. They were all she had.

The front door slammed shut and she rested her head against Royce's chest.

'You're good at this.'

'What?'

'Comfort. Reassurance.' Rachel looked up at him. 'What do you do back in

Nashville? Let me guess — you're a priest, or maybe a counsellor?'

'I was a dentist.'

'A dentist? But you never said.'

'You never asked.' He shrugged. 'Don't tell me you've got a dental phobia as well as a Santa one?'

'I do not . . . Oh, very smart. Distracting me won't work.' It suddenly clicked that he'd spoken in the past tense. 'What do you do now you've stopped filling teeth?'

A flush of heat tinged his skin.

'I want to make a living by writing. I've been working on some poetry and short stories.' He stared down at his hands.

'My folks think I'm nuts. Dad believes the world begins and ends with a dentist's chair and Mom backs him all the way.' Royce's bitterness was clear. 'We're not exactly talking much at the moment.'

His obsession with Christmas made more sense now.

'For the record I don't think you're nuts.'

'Thanks.' Royce stroked his warm hand against her cheek. 'I've wanted a

50

proper conversation with you for days but I'm guessing we should . . .'

Horror ran through her.

'I'm chatting to you as though I don't have a care in the world . . .'

'Go easy on yourself.' He checked his watch. 'How about going to the hospital before Mollie gets out of school to have a quick word with Anna's doctor? Sorry. I shouldn't assume . . . Do you want me to come with you?'

'Oh, yes. Would you?'

An hour later she confirmed with Anna's medical team that keeping the news of Harry's disappearance a secret was their best move, at least for the time being. She hoped Harry and Anna would forgive her.

'Can you go through with this?' Royce asked.

'Yes, with your help.'

'You've got it.'

'Let's go and have a chat with Anna as though nothing's wrong.' She plastered on a bright smile.

Hidden Talents

'Oh, Aunty Rach, they're awesome.' Mollie beamed. 'They're better than Mr Roy's.'

Royce winked over the little girl's head and Rachel struggled to keep a straight face.

'You'll hurt his feelings.'

Mollie's face dropped.

'Your aunt is teasing. She knows I'm a firm believer that if more people had awesome Christmas lights the world would be a better place.'

After their hospital visit Rachel's brave mask slipped when he suggested they test her outside lights.

'They're pathetic.' Rachel grimaced.

'No, they're just ... not enough,' Royce smiled.

'But I don't have time ...'

'I've got some spare lights in my garage plus a couple of inflatables I didn't have room for.'

'What a surprise.'

'Cheeky.'

He'd gathered everything together and given Rachel instructions how to inflate the snowman and Father Christmas.

'I'm off to the garden centre because I saw a neat family of wooden reindeer on sale. You can programme them to light up and dance to 'Rudolph the Red-nosed Reindeer'. Mollie will go nuts for them. I'll put up the lights when I get back.'

'Mollie, we need to get your costume ready for tomorrow but I promise when it's dark we'll come back out to admire the lights properly,' Rachel told her niece.

'What costume?' Royce asked.

'The angel one Mollie told me about when I picked her up after school today. It's for the Christmas pageant tomorrow morning.'

'Perhaps you could buy one in St Mervyn,' he suggested. 'Or cut holes in a sheet and tie a belt around the waist.'

'Yuck.' Mollie screwed up her face. Mummy always makes my costumes and they're always the best. I need white sparkly wings and a halo, too.'

Royce felt for the little girl but more so for Rachel, grey with strain underneath her fake smile.

'I'd be happy to help,' he offered.

'Is sewing another of your many talents?'

He ignored her sarcasm and smiled. In college he joined a drama group because he fancied Kylie Johnson, one of the leading actresses, and got stuck working backstage when they discovered he couldn't act to save his life.

He'd done everything from paint scenery to sourcing props and helped make costumes when the designer was swamped. They spent one whole weekend sewing 32 costumes for the ensemble characters in 'Les Miserables'. Yeah, he could sew.

'Fine.' She sighed. 'Come around for dinner at half past five and we'll see what we can come up with.' Rachel's eyes narrowed. 'And yes, I've got dinner covered.'

'Good — because I'm starving.' He'd hurry into town and pick up a few supplies. 'See ya later.'

Rachel watched his retreating figure with a sinking heart. She longed to crawl into bed and cry but giving in wasn't an option.

'Never is until the mission's over, sis. Then you give yourself a few moments to howl and mourn before knuckling down to the next task.'

These had been Harry's exact words once when she asked how he and his fellow soldiers coped. It was her job to support his wife, take care of his precious daughter and keep everything together until he made it safely back.

'Can we have fish fingers?' Mollie tugged her hand. 'Please.'

'How about we make pizza instead?'

When Rachel lived in Rome she'd begged Paolo at the local pizzeria to share his secrets and used them multiple times since to surprise a few people. Of course, when they discovered pizza was the only recipe in her repertoire it wasn't quite as impressive.

'Will it be better than fish fingers?'

The limited offerings she'd fed Mollie over the last few days didn't encourage confidence in her culinary skills.

'I promise it'll be awesome.'

Mollie frowned.

'Mummy buys frozen pizza or a man brings it in a box.'

Rachel suppressed the urge to throw a fist in the air. Finally! Something she could do better than Anna. She shouldn't be so pleased but was only human.

A few minutes later the kitchen looked as though a flour volcano had erupted. Mollie had dabs of pizza dough all over her face and in her hair but also the biggest smile on her face.

'Now we put the dough in a warm place to rise and leave it until it's twice this size.' By her calculations it should be ready to roll out, add the toppings and pop in the oven as Royce arrived.

'It doesn't look like pizza.' Mollie's scepticism returned.

'Do you trust me?'

'Yeees.' The long, dragged-out reply wasn't a ringing endorsement.

With the little girl settled in front of the TV watching her favourite wildlife show Rachel finished clearing up as the doorbell rang.

'Here's your angel-making service. Am I at the right house?' Royce breezed in, his arms loaded with boxes and bags. He popped a surprise kiss on Rachel's cheek before she could move away. 'You must be the would-be angel.'

'Don't be silly, Mr Roy. Aunty Rach isn't going to be in the school play — I am.' Mollie put him right.

'We could make your aunt a halo, too, and a set of wings. She could wear them when she watches your play.'

'Stop it, you pair,' Rachel intervened. 'Let's get the pizzas made and we'll work on your costume after we've eaten.'

Royce mouthed an apology and she couldn't stay mad. What sort of man willingly helped out this way? A good one.

For all she knew he had a wife and kids back in Nashville. She'd never asked and he hadn't said. Of course, he hadn't asked her any personal questions either but they weren't seeing each other 'that way' so it didn't matter.

Don't look at me that way, Royce thought. Your eyes are shining and there's a fleck of flour on your cheek. I can't tell you how beautiful you are with Mollie standing there, but one day I will.

'I'm sorry, did you say something?' He snapped out of his daydream.

'I said there's beer in the fridge if you want to help yourself while we work our pizza magic.'

He sat out of the way while they divided the dough, rolled it out and shaped it into two pizzas. Mollie concentrated on placing cubes of ham and grated cheese on hers while Rachel worked on theirs. Royce almost choked on his beer when he saw Rachel slicing eggs.

'Um, that's unusual. Where did you get that idea from?'

'A pizzeria on the outskirts of Rome.' She grinned. 'I made friends with the chef and his specialty was a pizza with spinach, prosciutto and sliced egg.

There's no tomato sauce but when the pizza comes out of the oven you sprinkle it with grated parmesan and a drizzle of olive oil. It became my favourite.'

'Why don't you stick with that for ours?'

'What a great idea.' Her wry response made him chuckle.

Ten minutes later they ate the best pizza he'd ever tasted.

'It's better from the Italian super hot old brick ovens. You should go there,' she said.

'It's on my wish list.' And so are you, he added silently as he looked into her eyes. A deep blush flooded her face and Royce's cheeks burned as well. 'Let's wash the dishes then we'll fix up our angel.' He ruffled Mollie's hair.

'Don't worry about the dishes. I'd rather get on with the costume.'

'Does Anna have a sewing machine?'

'Yes, but I . . .'

'How about any white material, maybe a nightdress or something you think she won't mind us using?'

59

'Probably.'

'Find that if you would and a couple of wire coat hangers.' Rachel opened her mouth to protest but swiftly shut it. 'Mollie, show me where your mom's sewing machine is.' He hauled all the supplies he'd brought up the stairs and went in the spare bedroom to check out the machine.

'Will this work?' Rachel handed him a white cotton floor-length sun dress with flounces around the neckline and hem.

'Perfect. First we need to measure Mollie then I'll get the wings made far enough for the two of you to work on decorating them.'

He tossed her a tape measure and wrote down the numbers as Rachel read them off. With the coat hangers fashioned into the shape of two wings he glued white gauzy material over them.

'Can I trust you with my glue gun?'

'Depends. Crafts aren't my thing.'

'Spread out an old sheet and sit on the floor.' Royce emptied out a pile of large white feathers on the bed.

'Mollie can pass them to you. Glue the feathers on in angled rows starting at the bottom so they hang down properly when you're done. I've got a ton of sparkly stuff to add later.' The little girl beamed.

'What are you going to do?'

'Make Mollie's dress.'

Rachel's dismissive snort made it clear she thought he'd bitten off more than he could chew. Apart from occasionally glancing over to see they were doing OK, he unpicked the dress and got busy.

'Good grief — you meant it.' The awe in Rachel's voice made him laugh. It was sewing, not rocket science.

'Lots of men sew. It's not a big deal.' Royce finished the hem and cut the thread. 'I bet your brother can sew. He can't rely on Anna when he's stuck in the wilds of Afghanistan and loses a button.' The light left her eyes and he rushed on.

'I've got silver trim and sparkles still to add but what do you think so far, Mollie?'

'Wow. That's so cool.' Mollie bounced

up and down. 'I want to try it on now.'

'Hang on a few minutes.' He used the glue gun for the embellishments, purposely overdoing it because an angel could never have too many sparkles. 'Put it on and come back to show me.'

His throat tightened at the sight of Mollie when she returned. For a quick job the costume fitted perfectly and he gruffly ordered her to turn around while he fixed on the wings.

'One halo coming up.' Royce fashioned pipe cleaners, silver stars and more feathers into a halo and attached it to a silver headband. 'Take a look.'

She did a happy twirl.

'It's awesome.' Mollie flung her arms around him and Royce gently patted her back, unable to speak. Behind her shoulder he spotted Rachel wiping away tears.

'Let Aunty Rach help you get ready for bed while I clear up. I'll fix our hot chocolate because my tummy tells me it's that time of day.'

Would Rachel feel up to talking later? He crossed his fingers.

Kisses and Confessions

Rachel didn't draw the living-room curtains, soothed by the flickering reflections from the coloured Christmas lights outside.

'Sit with me?' Royce's gentle request warmed her heart. Confidence didn't need to be shouted aloud and masculinity wasn't proved by pushing other people around.

She joined him on the sofa and snuggled closer when he draped his arm around her shoulders.

'I can't thank . . .'

'Then don't,' Royce whispered. 'Seeing Mollie happy . . .' His raspy voice betrayed his own emotions. It had been a long hard day.

'If you aren't busy in the morning would you come with me to the school play? It starts at ten.'

'Are you sure? Isn't it only for family?' Rachel frowned.

'Right now Mollie's a bit short on the

family front. We're the best she's got.'

'In that case, count me in.'

'You can help make sure I don't mess up taking a video and pictures to show Anna — and Harry when he comes back.' Her confidence wavered. 'If he . . .'

'Shush.' Royce rested his hand on hers. 'He needs us to be positive. It's like believing in Santa Claus, or y'all's Father Christmas, it all comes down to faith.

'Humanity isn't all bad. Maybe Harry's injured and being taken care of by a poor Afghan family happy to share the little they have with a man who is trying his best to help their country.'

'But what if the enemy captured him? The Taliban is ruthless.'

'Then we hope to goodness they show him some mercy.' A hard edge crept into his voice. 'We've got to concentrate on fighting his battle here and trust the rest will be taken care of.'

Rachel grasped his face with both hands and gave him a swift, hard kiss, tasting the lingering sweetness of chocolate on his lips.

'That's for being a good man.'

'They say good guys finish last where women are concerned but if that's what I get for being last I'm in.'

She waited for him to kiss her back.

'What's wrong?'

'Am I taking advantage?'

'What of?'

'You,' he murmured. 'You're paddling like crazy to stay afloat with all this plus it's been one heck of a day and you've gotta be wiped out.'

'Oh, Royce, there's being good and there's . . .'

'Being a wimp?'

'No,' Rachel assured him. 'You're definitely not one of those. If you were I wouldn't be . . . attracted to you.'

'Attracted?' A satisfied smile deepened his laughter lines. 'That sounds mighty good from where I'm sitting.'

Before she could tell him not to get too full of himself Rachel found herself being thoroughly kissed.

'Mmm, I was right. Mighty good.' He kissed her again until the temperature in the room soared to heat wave levels. 'I guess we ought to talk.'

Royce eased away and she fought against pouting, feeling rather like Mollie after being told she must stop playing with her favourite toy and do her homework instead.

'OK?'

'I suppose.' Rachel smoothed out her creased skirt and crossed her hands on her lap while trying to look pleased.

'That doesn't work when Mollie does it, either.' The innocent look she tossed his way made Royce roar with laughter. 'You're a real pickle.' Her wrinkled-up nose made him laugh harder. 'Never been called one of those before? It means being a weird person.'

'You're calling me weird?' She pulled the string to light up the nutcracker on his jumper. 'At least my clothes can't be mistaken for gaudy holiday decorations.'

'They're part of my attraction.'

'You're probably right.' Rachel gave him a quizzical look. 'I could say you've got nice eyes and a gorgeous smile plus

66

you're intelligent and good humoured but let's be honest,' she playfully batted her eyelashes, 'it's really your outlandish fashion choices that won my heart.'

She turned the same colour as a regulation British post-box, making him guess that the last three words popped out before her brain engaged her mouth in gear.

'I thought so.' He'd leave it for now because there were other more important questions he wanted answered.

'Go on, ask away.'

'Have you got a crystal ball tucked away somewhere?'

'You didn't realise you were that obvious?'

His folks always claimed they never knew what he was thinking but Rachel didn't have any problem.

'Scary, isn't it?'

'Yep.'

'I'll help you out.' Without any visible sign of emotion she started to talk about her childhood.

'When I was fifteen and Harry was

thirteen our family shattered. I know middle-aged healthy people die of the flu every winter but they were my parents and I loved them.' Her voice broke. 'Very much.'

'How did you manage?'

'We moved in with our gran in St Mervyn but her knees were bad so I pretty much took care of us and did all the housework.

'I scraped by at school but I delayed my university place until after Harry joined the army.' For a few seconds she looked unbearably sad.

'That's why I prefer to keep people at a distance these days. Loving is too . . . hard. Harry and his family wriggled into my heart but I even fight that.' She dredged up a wry smile. 'At least I did until this week.'

'And me?'

'You?' Rachel rolled her eyes. 'I've no idea what to do with you. You're more stubborn than they are.'

He took that as a compliment.

'What's next on Mollie's list?' The

abrupt change of topic surprised her but the last thing she needed tonight was a serious conversation about where their 'attraction' might lead. Maybe he wasn't ready for it, either.

'Thankfully it's something I know how to do for a change. Ice skating.' Tears shimmered in her eyes.

'Mollie asked why I taught her dad to skate which means Harry never talked about my history or our parents.'

'That hurts.'

'Yes. They were wonderful people and would've doted on her.' Rachel's cheeks heated. 'I suppose he had his reasons but if . . . when . . . he comes home I need to talk to him about it.'

Negotiating the delicate subject of parents wasn't Royce's area of expertise and as an only child he retained a sort of detached curiosity when it came to the topic of siblings.

'Every winter there's an ice skating rink at the Eden project near St Austell.

'When Mollie gets out of school after the play tomorrow my plan is to come home here for lunch and make it to Eden by one o'clock.

'I've booked us in for one of the general skating sessions starting on the hour and lasting forty minutes — that'll be long enough for her.' Rachel grinned. 'You're welcome to come with us.'

'Uh, thanks — but I'll sit this one out. I tried skating once and spent most of the time flat on my backside. I was bruised for weeks.' He gave her a shrewd look. 'Something tells me you're good.'

'I was.' A shadow flitted across her smile. 'There used to be rink in Truro that was open year round and my sweet father drove me there at the crack of dawn three times a week for lessons before school.

'Our weekends were totally consumed by my skating too because I got into the competition circuit and was doing pretty well until . . .' Rachel shrugged.

'You've never picked it up again?'

'I needed a steady job and I had a knack for computers. Getting into the IT field made sense.'

'Couldn't you have kept it as a hobby?' Royce kicked himself for being so stupid. Dabbling in something she'd excelled at would drive her crazy. 'Forget it. I'm dumb.'

'No, not dumb. Some things simply are.'

He'd never been one to accept the idea of karma.

'I'm excellent at my job. Only the elite few make a successful career out of figure skating and it's doubtful I'd have been one of them.'

'But you'll always wonder.'

'No, I stopped doing that a long time ago.' She smiled. 'It's getting late.'

'Wow, she can tell the time, too. Amazing.'

'Don't be like this,' Rachel pleaded.

'Then let me in.'

'I can't.'

'Can't or won't?' A sensible man would cut his losses until they both calmed down but the stubborn streak he inherited from his father reasserted itself. 'Think about it. Think about it real hard.'

'Shall I add it to the long list of worries keeping me awake at night?'

Royce burned with shame.

'Sorry. I don't know what got into me.'

'Just go.' She pushed a lock of hair away from her eyes exposing her thin, tired face. 'I can't deal with this today.'

'I know. I tried to tell you I'm not always a good man but you wouldn't listen.' His lame attempt at humour failed. 'I guess I'll say goodnight and be off.'

'Goodnight.'

When he stepped outside, the sight of the singing, dancing reindeer didn't improve his mood. If he wasn't careful he'd become a bona fide grouch, too.

The Play's the Thing

'Why can't I ask Mr Roy to come to my play? All my friends have lots of people coming and I've only got you.' Mollie pushed her cereal around the bowl and jabbed hard enough to make a spoonful of frosted bears topple out on the table.

'He's busy.' Rachel's head throbbed. She stayed awake worrying about Harry all night and shot out of bed when the phone rang at seven o'clock this morning.

The no-news-is-good-news update from the family liaison officer should have been a relief but the strain was getting to her. Today meant another visit to Anna and another lie.

'After you finish school we'll have fun and do today's Christmas wish.' Mollie stopped poking the soggy mound of cereal.

'Meeting Father Christmas and petting a reindeer?'

Rachel hadn't worked out the logistics

of that request yet.

'Um no, I'm saving that for another day.' She pushed the leaflet about the Eden skating rink across the table.

'Ice skating? Yippee!'

'It's hard. You'll fall down a lot today but if you like it we can go again and you'll get better.'

Anna and Harry might not thank her if Mollie fell in love with it but she would take that chance. 'It takes a lot of practice.'

Her warning didn't dent Mollie's enthusiasm and her niece chattered away about being able to go skating with her dad. Rachel hoped so. She plastered on a smile and last night's conversation with Royce returned to haunt her.

'Can you go through with this?' he'd asked.

'Yes, with your help.'

'You've got it.'

Why did she push him away? Doing this alone was daunting.

'You need to get ready for school while I'll make sure we've got everything for your angel costume. Make sure you . . .'

'Brush my teeth. Comb my hair. Put on my shoes and coat.' Mollie recited the list she must have heard hundreds of times from Anna.

'Perfect.' Rachel's admiration for her sister-in-law had grown in leaps and bounds over the last week.

Somehow they made it out of the door with five minutes to spare. Outside the school gates she tried to stop Mollie grabbing the bag with her angel costume.

'I'll take it in to your teacher. Some of the other mums are.'

'I can do it myself,' Mollie insisted. 'Anyway, you're not my mum.' The throwaway comment wasn't said unkindly but still hurt. 'Bye.' She raced off with a happy wave.

'Independent little soul, isn't she?' The tousled blonde in faded jeans and a baggy grey sweatshirt standing nearby smiled over.

'Uh, yes.' This was the first time anyone had spoken beyond a casual hello. She assumed everyone else knew each other and huddled in their little groups, not out of unfriendliness but habit.

'It's Rachel Trewarren, right? I remember you. We were at school together.'

'Were we?'

'Pansy Hawken. I was a Budge before I married.' Pansy laughed. 'I also had buck teeth, bad skin and definitely wasn't a blonde.'

'It's coming back. I haven't been . . . around here much in a long time so I'm out of touch.'

Pansy nodded towards the other parents.

'People wanted to speak to you but they weren't sure . . .' Her voice trailed away. 'Are you coming back for the play later?'

'Wouldn't miss it for the world.' Rachel checked her watch. 'I'd better go — I've a few things to do beforehand.'

'Me, too. I need to change into my Christmas jumper.' Pansy grinned. 'Jilly will be embarrassed but she'll get over it.' Her gaze slid over Rachel's fitted black coat, leggings and black boots. 'Most people wear Christmassy bits of some sort or other.'

Royce would be the star of the show if he turned up. But he wouldn't now because she had sent him off with a flea in his ear for puncturing her safe little bubble.

'That's not really me.'

'No. I can see that.'

She heated under her old friend's scrutiny.

'How is poor Anna? It can't be much fun being stuck in the hospital but I suppose it's for the best.'

Rachel satisfied Pansy's curiosity and slipped in a mention that Harry would hopefully be home soon. If his disappearance leaked into the press it would be an absolute nightmare.

'See you later.' She made a quick retreat.

* * *

Reindeer with jingle bells around their necks or the fat, jolly Father Christmas?

Royce tugged the reindeer jumper off the hanger. He'd ignore his disagreement with Rachel and go to the school play because Mollie deserved all the support they could give her.

'Being a dad's a hundred times more frightening than facing the Taliban. The sole responsibility for this human being lies with you and if you mess up . . .'

Harry made that confession a few days before he left for Afghanistan and it stayed with Royce.

Despite a difficult relationship with his own parents, he still wanted to be a father one day.

Until now he'd never met a woman he wanted to build a life with although after only a matter of days he shouldn't even consider Rachel in that light.

Beyond the fact she was smart, attractive and hated Christmas what did he really know about her? The few snippets she'd revealed about her family?

He tried to tell himself the kisses they shared were simply 'friendly' but they hadn't felt that way.

Royce popped the small presents he'd picked up for Mollie into a shiny red bag under a mass of silver tissue paper.

He spotted Rachel emerge from her front door and march off down the road. If he hurried he'd easily catch up with her but arriving at the school separately denied her the opportunity to send him away without making a fuss.

At the school he easily spotted Rachel in the packed assembly hall. Everyone else wore colourful Christmas clothes whereas she was chic as ever in her habitual black.

Before anyone else claimed the seat next to her, Royce wended his way through the crowd of people and tapped her shoulder.

'Are you saving this for anyone?'

'Oh, it's you.' A brief flash of annoyance was replaced by a hint of amusement as he shrugged off his green quilted jacket. 'I might have known you'd . . .'

'Turn up? Wear another tacky jumper?'

'Yes and yes.'

'I'll go away again if you want?'

'You might as well stay now you're here.' Rachel exhaled a weary sigh. 'Mollie will be happy. She wanted to ring you this morning.' A tinge of heat framed her cheekbones. 'I lied and told her you were busy.'

'I can be, if you prefer?'

'Oh, sit down.'

He ignored the unenthusiastic response and joined her. Black clothes didn't flatter the tired shadows under her eyes but in his opinion she was lovelier than any other woman in the room.

'Any news?'

'No. The liaison officer rang but . . . there's nothing new. I'm taking Mollie ice skating after lunch.'

'She'll love that.'

'I doubt it. She'll fall down continually and complain of the cold.'

'Did you the first time?'

Rachel shook her head.

'I picked it up like that.' She clicked her fingers. 'Not like Harry. He was capable of getting from point A to point B without falling but that's about all you can say.'

'I bet she takes after you.'

A loud bell clanged and everyone fell quiet as the curtains opened.

'Oh.' Rachel gasped. Mollie stood alone at the front of the stage with her feathered wings and glittery halo sparkling under the spotlight.

Royce slipped out his phone to do the best he could without blocking anyone else's view. Mollie introduced the play like a seasoned professional before disappearing into the wings for the first act to begin.

'I thought a small group of angels were speaking together.' She brushed at her eyes. 'The little minx.'

'Can't imagine who she gets that from.' Royce earned a dig in the ribs for his cheek. There was the usual mixture of children forgetting their lines, one young shepherd tripped over his too-long costume and the bossy Virgin Mary bopped Joseph on the head when he tucked the Jesus baby doll under his arm like a rugby ball.

When the play finished, the hall became a mass of over-excited children searching for their families.

'You came!' Mollie flung herself at him, red-faced with happiness and with one wing drooping precariously.

'I couldn't miss seeing my star angel, could I? You were awesome.'

'I remembered all the words.'

'Hi, Rachel.' Pansy wriggled her way through the crowd. 'Mollie did an amazing job. Her mum and dad would be so proud.' Tears welled in the woman's eyes. 'It's awful about Harry. Everyone's devastated.'

'What on earth do you mean?'

'It's all over the news. Didn't you . . .'

Royce squeezed Rachel's shoulder. 'Why don't you chat to your friend outside where you can hear yourselves talk?' He managed to smile at Mollie.

'I've got something special for our star.' The red gift bag dangled from his fingers. 'Let's sit down and you can open it.'

He turned away from the stunned

shock on Rachel's face. Right now his job was to shield the little girl from the possibility that her world could have shattered into a million pieces.

A Long Story

Pansy shuffled from one foot to the other and avoided Rachel's gaze.

'What precisely did you hear?'

'I assumed you . . .'

Rachel's patience balanced on a knife edge.

'Pansy. Exactly what you heard. Please.'

'They're saying on the news that Harry is missing, presumed dead. Something to do with an ambush.'

Later Rachel would wonder how she managed to stay calm and explain the whole story to Pansy.

'I would be the first to know if there'd been any fresh information.' But would she? She switched her phone on vibrate when she arrived at school and tucked it away in her bag.

What if Anna watched the news or listened to the radio? She dragged out her mobile and found three missed calls from Captain Worthing. Everything blurred and she vaguely heard someone repeating her name over and over.

'Are you all right?' Pansy's anxious face came back into focus. 'Sorry. Of course you're not.'

'You'll have to excuse me. I must listen to these messages.' She managed to walk all the way around the corner of the building before collapsing against the wall. After taking a few steadying breaths she pressed the button.

Tears ran down her face listening to Amy's words and a wave of relief surged through her.

The army had received new information from a local shepherd who swore he'd seen an injured soldier limping into a cave but was too scared to approach the man.

Without going into specifics Amy said the searchers checked out the area and found evidence of a possible link with Harry. The liaison officer's last message contained an apology.

The news of Harry's disappearance had leaked out through the family of another soldier in his unit and been distorted along the way. Amy picked up Rachel's call on the first ring.

'I'm happy to come back to St Kellow. We contacted the hospital with an update and by now they should have moved Anna into a private ward using the excuse it'll be more restful for her.

'They've asked the staff not to talk about the situation in front of her and to be on the watch for any journalists who might try to sneak in.

'Her doctor conceded that Anna needs to know what's happening now the news has broken and we could speak with her together if you prefer?'

'That's OK — I think it'll come better from me.' Rachel sighed. 'I'll get over to the hospital right away.' She decided to see Pansy before she left because her talkative old friend would spread the correct information around faster than the BBC.

'Aunty Rach, where were you?' Mollie raced towards her with Royce striding along behind. She hoped her half-smile hinted that the news wasn't as bad as they'd feared. 'Mr Roy gave me a bag of awesome Christmas biscuit cutters, only he's funny and calls them cookie cutters. I've got a snowman and Father Christmas and reindeer and lots of neat stuff.'

'That's lovely, sweetheart.' She crouched in front of her niece. 'There's been a change of plans . . .'

'Your aunt found out the ice skating rink is really busy today,' Royce interrupted, 'and thought tomorrow would be better. Would you like to come over and bake cookies with me this afternoon while Aunty Rach visits your mommy?' He touched Rachel's arm. 'If that's OK?'

She nodded, overwhelmed by his thoughtfulness.

'But I want to see Mummy, too,' Mollie whined.

'She's tired today,' Rachel said. 'The babies kept her awake last night. If we visit her tomorrow you can tell her about going ice skating.'

'And take her some cookies,' Royce suggested. 'We could make enough to give to the nurses and doctors, too. Would you like that? You could wear your angel costume.'

'Cool.'

Rachel had never met such a sweet man. A sweet man who kissed like a distinctly un-sweet one. The perfect combination.

Rachel spotted Mollie's teacher heading their way and desperately wanted to avoid a conversation about Harry.

'Let's go home.'

'I need to change my shoes,' Mollie protested. 'They'll get dirty and wet.'

'I'll carry you.' Royce swept her up in one arm. 'Sooner we get out of here the better,' he muttered.

'Mind reader.'

'I try.'

They couldn't say much more with Mollie listening to every word. Rachel walked quietly beside him and barely paid any attention to the animated discussion about what kind of biscuits to make.

Amy Worthing was evasive when she

asked what they found in the cave which could be for security reasons but were there indications Harry was badly hurt or worse.

'Damn.' Royce's soft curse brought her attention back.

'Mr Roy said a naughty word.'

'I'm sorry, kiddo, but . . .' He grimaced and nodded towards the turning for Poltair Road where a jumble of cars and vans, including several with TV antennas, were parked all along the road.

Royce whipped around before Mollie could see anything and Rachel's stomach churned.

'How about we play a game and pretend there are biscuit cutter thieves looking for us?' Royce set the little girl back down and continued his rambling story while he removed Mollie's wings and draped his coat around her shoulders.

'We need to disguise you. Let's change your shoes in case we need to make a run for it. There's a secret way to reach my house and we'll use that.'

'This is fun,' Mollie squealed and clasped the red bag to her chest, her eyes flashing with determination.

Rachel probably wasn't thrilled with his desperate storyline but she didn't protest. One day he discovered the narrow lane running behind Poltair Road was accessible from Trebah Avenue, the next street over.

His back garden didn't have a gate into the lane but the low wooden fence should be easy enough to climb. Hopefully the press weren't smart enough to figure that out.

'Follow me.' He set off and as they reached the lane Royce held up a finger to his mouth to stop Mollie chattering. 'Rachel, I'll climb over first then you pass Mollie to me and come across yourself.'

'Uh, my trousers are a bit on the tight side.'

Royce gamely suppressed a chuckle. 'I'll help you.' Her blush deepened. A few minutes later the only casualty was Rachel's dignity after he hauled her across the fence like a sack of potatoes.

'Let's get inside . . .'

'Before the biscuit-cutter thieves spot us.' Mollie almost burst with excitement as she tiptoed across the grass.

'How about changing out of your angel clothes so you don't get them messed up when we're baking?' he suggested when they were safely in his kitchen.

'I'll help,' Rachel offered.

'I'm not a baby.'

Royce kept a straight face.

'Of course you aren't, kiddo. The restroom . . . I mean the guest loo is out that door.' He pointed across to the hall. 'It's straight in front of you.'

'I still think . . .'

He shushed Rachel with a swift kiss.

'She's not a baby and anyway I need you to myself.'

'Oh.'

Royce wrapped his arms around her and she clung on to him, pouring out the whole worrying story about Harry. He wouldn't lie and promise that everything would be all right.

'How can I get to the hospital with

those vultures outside?'

'Easy. You pop on a disguise and I'll call a cab. There's no reason for the press to be interested in someone getting in a taxi from their neighbour's house.' Rachel didn't look convinced. 'How about some lunch first?'

'I couldn't eat.'

'I'll find something for you to wear.'

'Good luck,' Rachel said wryly.

Honey, the good luck already happened when you walked into my life, Royce thought. The rest is gravy or icing depending on whether you're a savoury or sweet lover. With me it's icing all the way — dentist or no dentist.

Each time she convinced herself that simply being friends with Royce was a perfectly reasonable aspiration he did this to her.

It wasn't so much what he said in his smooth, deep drawl, but more what he expressed through his unflinching gaze. His eyes darkened, laced through with a quiet longing that made her skin tighten and her heart race.

'I'm starving.' Mollie zoomed back into the kitchen.

'There's plenty of food in the fridge and pantry. Help yourselves while I rustle up some clothes for your aunt.'

'One sandwich coming up.'

'Here you go. This should do the trick.' Royce thrust a pile of clothes on the table and she spotted a gaudy Christmas jumper in the mix.

Five minutes later she scowled in the mirror. She'd get her revenge for this. The fluffy green and red jumper, decorated with an elf face that could only be described as manic, grazed her knees and tiny green felt feet dangled from the hem.

Thankfully he hadn't found a colourful alternative to her black trousers. Rachel dragged on the red and white striped pointy hat complete with a tinkling bell.

'Aunty Rach, why are you wearing silly clothes?'

'Because we're still playing our game,' Royce answered for her.

If the imaginary biscuit-cutter thieves were on the lookout for a smart, dark-haired woman dressed all in black these ridiculous clothes should fool them and hopefully the same went for journalists.

'I'm off to see your mummy. Shall I give her a hug from you?'

'Yes, please. And give the babies one, too.'

Rachel came perilously close to crying until Royce rested his warm hand across her back.

'I will. Be good and save some biscuits for me.'

'You'll do fine,' Royce whispered out by the door. 'Did I tell you I've got a thing about elves?'

'Why doesn't that surprise me?' She flounced off before he could reply.

Naturally her taxi driver treated her to every Christmas joke he knew and it worsened when she arrived at the hospital.

Rachel endured a lot of giggles and finger pointing, plus a few questionable offers connected with ringing her bell.

She dived into the ladies' loos and ripped off the hat but combing her hair didn't do much to improve her appearance.

Outside Anna's new room she plastered on a smile before pushing open the door.

'There you are at last.' Anna awkwardly pulled herself up in the bed. 'I want a straight answer about what's going on.

'No-one will talk to me about anything more serious than what I want for my tea.' She glared.

'They moved me from a lovely friendly ward to this isolation cell and apparently the telly and the radio are both broken.' Her hands rested on top of her ballooning stomach.

'If Harry is dead you've got to tell me. I've got the right to know.'

'Harry's not dead, at least not as far as we're aware.' Rachel perched on the end of the bed and explained everything while Anna bit back tears but never broke down.

'Can you forgive us? We were only

thinking of you and the babies.'

'It may take me a while.' Anna's eyes glittered. 'In the meantime why don't you tell me why my sophisticated sister-in-law who usually passes for a native Frenchwoman is dressed like a drunken elf?'

'It's a long story.'

'I'm not going anywhere, am I?'

This was part of her penance. Anna was an incurable romantic and would have her married off to Royce before the day was over.

No False Promises

Royce dried his hands before answering the door to a bedraggled elf. The rain hadn't done Rachel any favours and his soaking wet jumper drooped pitifully towards the floor.

'Is Anna . . .'

'All right? Not really but she took the news stoically and she's still speaking to me.' She dragged off the soggy hat. 'At least this ridiculous outfit made her laugh.'

'See, I'm good for something.'

'Maybe.' She sniffed the air. 'Some-one's been baking.'

One day he'd prove his talents extended beyond making gingerbread men and angel costumes but for now he'd feed her.

'Did you get any lunch?'

'No, but I really should take Mollie home. My first priority is a shower and clean clothes that don't drip when I walk. And before you ask how I got this wet I couldn't bear another humiliating taxi ride and catching the bus involved quite a walk on both ends.'

Listening to her story without laughing stretched his acting abilities to the limit.

'But wasn't it worse having a bus load of people rag you instead of one driver?'

'You forget it's nearly Christmas. I blended in with all the other nutcases out there. Ugly jumper office parties are popular this year and several people suggested I'd have won with this . . . thing.'

'I'm gonna take that as a compliment.'

'You would.'

He ignored the dig.

'Mollie fell asleep watching TV. Why don't you pop next door and get . . . de-elfed? The people who lived in these two houses must've been good friends or there wouldn't be a gate between our two gardens. No climbing required.' Royce stifled a smile. 'Off you go before you catch pneumonia.' He shooed her out of the door.

What made her borrow one of Anna's blouses? The pale grey silk blouse shot through with fine sapphire blue threads wasn't the last word in Christmas cheer but compared to her black turtleneck could be considered reckless.

Two years living in Paris had cemented Rachel's natural inclination towards simple, elegant clothes and she'd settled into an almost unbroken year-round version of many Frenchwomen's 'you-can-never-go-wrong-with-black' wardrobe.

The blouse worked well with a slim, knee length skirt of buttery black suede, opaque black tights and soft black leather ankle boots.

She poked around Anna's make-up drawer and selected a deep pink lipstick to try. An improvement on her normal barely tinted lip gloss, the warmer colour did something unexpected for her. Rachel brushed her freshly washed hair, foregoing the gel she used to slick it back.

Why she was doing all this? The

simple answer was Royce Carver. None of the men she'd dated over the years ever affected her deeply until Harry's crazy neighbour smiled at her over a mug of hot chocolate.

His outlandish Christmas jumpers, unruly hair and soft, deep drawl added to his appeal but it was his kindness that sealed the deal.

In today's world that seemed an increasingly rare commodity. Maybe she'd been spoiled by her own father and Harry but if that was the case she didn't care.

Royce flung open the door before she could knock and there was a gleam in his deep green eyes.

'Wow, don't you clean up good?'

Rachel had received more flowery compliments in her time but this was genuine. Over his shoulder she spotted Mollie barrelling towards them. If she didn't get this man on his own soon . . .

'Aunty Rach, you've got to come in the kitchen and see our Christmas biscuits.' She tugged on her hand. 'They're the best ever. Hurry up.'

When Royce gave a tiny shrug her spirits soared. They were on the same page.

'Do you like sugary ones or gingerbreads?' Mollie chattered away. 'You can have one of each. I did. And Mr Roy made ones that tasted funny but he said you'd eat them.'

'Funny?'

'They're an Italian Christmas specialty made with anise, lemon and ricotta.' He tilted his engaging smile her way. 'I guessed they might . . .'

'Be some of my favourite flavours? You're spot on.' Anyone would think she'd given him a million pounds by the grin splitting his face in two. 'Lead me to them.'

'He says you've got to eat boring soup first like we had to.'

'Oh, really?'

'Yes, really.' Royce nodded his agreement. 'You've eaten nothing decent all day and I don't want you fading away through a lack of proper nutrition.'

'You sound like my . . . mother.' Over the years she'd perfected the art of rarely mentioning her parents.

'You have a mummy?' Mollie asked. 'Is she as nice as my mummy?'

Royce cupped her shoulders with his strong, warm hands. No-one could force her to go along with Harry's choice not to talk about their parents. Her brother wasn't here and Rachel was tired of evading her niece's logical questions.

'Let's sit down and I'll tell you all about my mummy while I eat my soup. Then we'll dive into the biscuits.'

Royce set a steaming bowl of vegetable soup in front of her and a basket of crusty wheat rolls. An unexpected wave of emotion swept over her. She'd forgotten the joy of being part of a family and gathering for a meal ready to share stories about everyone's day.

Royce's compassionate gaze almost undid her but she forced down a few spoonfuls of soup.

'Homemade? It's delicious.'

'Yep. It's easy. You throw in whatever

is laying around the kitchen needing to be eaten up.'

That wouldn't work in her sterile Paris apartment with its half-empty fridge containing bottled water, fruit and low-fat yogurts.

'I'll take your word for it.' Rachel managed to eat about two-thirds before giving up. 'Mollie, you asked about my mummy. She was kind and very pretty.' She touched her niece's cheek. 'You look very much like her.'

'Why do I look like your mummy?'

The little girl wasn't old enough to make the connection.

'You know you'll be a big sister to the twins when they arrive?' Mollie nodded. 'I'm your daddy's big sister.'

'Oh.'

How could she explain about their parents' deaths without frightening Mollie?

No doubt this was why her normally fearless brother chickened out, especially given his dangerous job. She wished she'd never started this but at exactly that moment Royce gave her hand a comforting squeeze.

'Our mummy and daddy were a lot of fun and loved us very much.' Rachel blinked hard. 'They got sick and couldn't get well again.'

'Did they die like my guinea pig?'

'Yes, they did.'

Mollie crawled into her lap and wound her arms around Rachel's neck.

'You must've been sad. I cried when Sneezy died. Did you cry?'

She nodded, hearing Harry's anguished howl when she broke the news to him because her grandmother was too distraught at losing her only child.

'I don't want my mummy and daddy to get sick and die.'

'They won't. I . . .' the words 'I promise' stuck in her throat.

'They won't, Mollie.' Royce's quiet certainty did the trick and her niece jumped off her lap. 'Perhaps Aunty Rach has a photo of your grandparents she can show you?'

'I certainly do, when we go back home.'

'Good, now is it biscuit time?'

'It certainly is.' Rachel stood up. 'Show me everything you made while I was out.' She'd been too flustered to notice the massive display of biscuits spread out on parchment paper over the kitchen counters.

'Wow, that's amazing. You did all these?' She was no baker but recognised the huge amount of work involved. Gingerbread men and women with all the details picked out in intricate white icing, every one different.

They'd used the other new cutters to fashion Father Christmas, snowmen, Christmas trees and angels out of shortbread biscuits all iced in a rainbow of colours.

Then there were the Italian biscuits simply dusted with a sprinkling of icing sugar and lemon zest.

She spotted the odd one obviously made by Mollie, either misshapen with blobs of smeared icing or in the case of the gingerbread people with the occasional arm or leg missing and Rachel loved that Royce hadn't put them to one side. She hugged Mollie.

'What a clever girl you are.' Recklessly she hugged Royce, too, and he held on a little longer than he should although not as long as she wanted.

'You're a very kind, clever man who prefers hiding his talents. I bet you're a great ice skater really.'

'No, I'm honestly not.' His face burned.

'Prove it. Go on. Come with us tomorrow.'

'Yes, yes, yes.' Mollie swung on his arm. 'I want you to and it's my Christmas wish list so you have to say yes.'

'In that case how can I refuse?' Royce's tight smile never reached his eyes.

'Are we ever going to eat any biscuits?' The complaint made them both laugh and Rachel's concern over the ice skating plans faded away, replaced by the onerous decision about which biscuit to try first.

Rekindling a Passion

Royce absentmindedly ate two more gingerbread men for breakfast along with a mug of strong coffee. How could he get out of the promise he'd made to Mollie without breaking his word? But was it worse to break his word or his leg — again?

In his nightmares he still heard the loud crack as his leg broke on contact with the ice after Johnny Rickard, the worst high school bully, pushed him out of the way. The memory made him feel dizzy and sick.

He'd woken up from surgery with metal plates and screws holding his leg together and endured four months of painful physiotherapy before walking anything close to normal.

The idea of strapping on skates again terrified him. Making himself think about Harry and the appalling situation he could be in now, if he was even still alive, should have put his fears into perspective but hadn't helped a whole lot.

The doorbell rang but the jangling sound of 'Hark! The Herald Angels Sing' couldn't cheer him up.

'My two favourite ladies.'

Mollie bounced around and an air of barely suppressed excitement emanated from Rachel.

'I want to see your dancing reindeer again!' Mollie exclaimed.

She left him alone with Rachel.

'Nice jumper.' She eyed up his jovial Father Christmas on skates.

'Yeah, right.' The edge to his voice made her frown. 'Don't pretend. We both know you think I'm tasteless and a bit nuts.'

'Why would you say that? What's up?' Her soft fingers brushed over his unshaven cheek. He'd been too nervous to trust himself with a razor. 'You aren't the type of man to fuss about being out-skated by a woman or a small child, and you certainly don't care what people think of your wacky jumpers so what's the problem? You'll make Mollie happy and we'll have a bit of a laugh.'

'Oh yeah? I doubt you'll be laughing when I'm carted off in an ambulance.' Before he knew where he was he'd confessed the whole pitiful story.

'You silly man.' Her slim hands cupped his face and he couldn't avoid her mesmerising eyes. 'That's sensible, not cowardly. Anyone with metal plates and pins holding their leg together shouldn't be on a skating rink. It's asking for trouble.'

'I hate to let Mollie down.'

'You won't be. We'll explain about your leg and you can still come along to watch and cheer us on . . . if you want to.' Rachel coloured up. 'I'm not being pushy, am I?'

'I sure hope you're not taking back the invitation because I'm happy to come.' He suspected he'd see another side to this interesting woman once she put on a pair of skates again.

Listening to her talk about ice skating he recognised the same intense fire he experienced when a piece of writing went well.

'If you want me?'

A broad smile lit her face and she treated him to a delicious kiss.

'Clear enough now?'

'Sure is.'

All the things they dared not put into words ricocheted between them.

'I'm ready to go now.' Mollie flung open the kitchen door. 'We'll be late.'

★ ★ ★

'Don't be too sad, Mr Roy.'

Rachel covered up a smile as they parked outside the Eden project. Her niece easily accepted Royce's explanation about why he couldn't join them skating.

'I'll get a kick out of watching you both.'

'Let's find where to get our skates, Mollie.'

The moment they stepped through the doors the cool rush of air brought back memories of her bleary-eyed father leaning on the barrier, as close to the rink as he could get, watching her early morning practice sessions.

She eyed the rental skates with distaste. Before she put them on Rachel knew they'd rub her feet. Years ago she became used to the comfort of custom made skates.

'They're too tight, Aunty Rach.' Mollie complained.

Carefully she explained that skates fitted differently from ordinary shoes. Too loose and they threw off a skater's balance.

'First we'll practise marching in small steps up and down the rubber carpet.'

'But everyone else is on the ice.'

Six-year-olds possessed limited patience but if she convinced Mollie to follow her advice the end result would be far fewer falls and a better all around experience.

'We'll pretend to be dinosaurs.' She coaxed her along and they practised it several times. 'Now we'll go on the ice. I know this sounds crazy but the first thing I'm going to teach you is how to fall because falling the proper way hurts a lot less.'

Holding her niece's hands she reminded her to take small, marching steps before they reached a good spot for their falls. Mollie drank in Rachel's words and could soon fall with the best of them.

'Now instead of loud marching steps, try to make them quiet and soon you'll find yourself gliding.'

'Look, I'm doing it!' Mollie yelled seconds before her feet went from under her and she fell smack on her bottom, forgetting everything Rachel taught her. An absolutely typical first attempt. Without any fuss she remembered the right way to stand back up.

'That's awesome.'

They skated for about 20 minutes before Rachel sensed Mollie was flagging. She didn't need to ask if her niece wanted to come back another day because a huge glow of pleasure lit up her face.

'We'll skate over to Mr Roy then it's time to go home for cookies and hot chocolate.' An unexpected pang knotted her stomach as a young man showed off near them, executing a couple of single axles followed by a double toe loop, not technically very well but good enough to make the other skaters stare admiringly in his direction.

'You did good, kiddo.' Royce high-fived Mollie over the railing. 'Why don't you come sit with me when you've got your skates off and we'll let Aunty Rach have a go on her own?'

'OK.'

'But she's tired, we ought . . .'

'There's fifteen minutes left in your time slot, it's a shame to waste it.'

They were equals when it came to persistence. She'd skate for a few minutes to placate him. Who was she trying to fool? She couldn't wait to see if the magic was still there.

Five minutes later she glided on to the ice and everything else faded away. In her head the canned Christmas music became the accompaniment to one of her favourite routines, Beethoven's 'Moonlight Sonata'.

Weaving through the noisy crowd Rachel became aware of people moving away. She tested herself with a few single axles before branching out a bit and surprised herself by landing every one spot on.

When the bell rang to signify the end of the session she could've screamed. Rachel nailed one last triple toe loop before skating to a halt in front of Royce and Mollie, registering the shock on his face and complete awe on her niece's.

She might not be able to bake fancy biscuits or run up an angel costume but teaching Mollie to skate — she'd aced that Christmas wish.

'Wow, Aunty Rach, you're the best skater in the whole world.'

Rachel could explain why that wasn't so or simply accept the compliment.

'I'm not really, sweetheart, but thank you.' A compromise. Rather like life. 'I'll take my skates back and meet you in the car.'

While she unlaced her skates an older man leaning heavily on a cane approached Rachel. His thick eyebrows and bright blue eyes ignited a spark of memory but for a few seconds she couldn't put a name with the face.

'Well, if it isn't little Rachel Trewarren. How are ye, lass?'

The moment she caught the heavy Irish accent it clicked. Despite his living here for at least 30 years nobody would ever have mistaken her old skating coach for a Cornishman.

'Mr Kelly? I don't believe it.'

'Oh, get on with you, lass. We're both old enough now for you to call me Paddy.'

From the time anyone recognised she wasn't a run of the mill seven-year-old hobby skater, this man was her mentor. At one point he tried to persuade her parents to let her move to Bristol for more intense training but they saw that as breaking up the family and refused.

In the end it didn't matter because she quit skating when her parents died and had never put on a pair of skates again until today.

'Are you still coaching?'

'I help out with skating classes every winter when this rink's open although it's a crying shame there's no year-round rink in Cornwall any longer.' He tapped his leg.

'My arthritis is bad after all those years on the ice.' Paddy studied her. 'You haven't skated in a while.'

'That obvious, is it?'

'To someone who knows you.' He gestured around the rink. 'They probably think you're an ex-Olympic champion.' Paddy's eyes narrowed. 'You could have been. I've only ever said that about two girls I trained.'

They both knew the other was Sophie Darling. British gold medallist in three successive Winter Olympics, star of a touring ice show and head judge on a popular TV ice skating competition.

They trained together for five years before Sophie's family moved to Bristol and then London to prepare her to compete nationally and internationally.

116

'I'm afraid I can't stay and chat. My niece and . . . a friend are waiting for me.'

'You'll be back?'

'This was Mollie's first time and she absolutely loved it so I'm sure we will.'

'I watched you with her and you've got the knack. You'd make a great coach.

'Come at six any weekday morning and you'll have the rink to yourself before classes start at seven. We don't open to the public until ten.' His eyes twinkled.

'And don't bother telling me you didn't hold on to your skates because I won't believe you.'

She hadn't opened the box containing all her skating memorabilia for close to 20 years. Rachel shifted it around with her from place to place before it ended up in Harry's attic when he settled in his new house.

'I'll think about your offer but I've got a lot going on.' Briefly she explained her situation.

'Skating is a great stress reliever. I'll be seeing you soon.' Paddy shooed her away without giving her the chance to contradict him.

Stirring up a passion she didn't have the time or inclination to allow back into her life wouldn't make things easier. She'd make up an excuse why it took her so long to return her skates. Paddy Kelly and Royce would be a lethal combination if they ganged up on her.

Faith and Hope

'Oh, you're early,' Rachel stammered.

'I didn't think ten minutes either way would matter. I'll go away again if you want?' Royce brandished a bottle of red wine. 'Unless this buys me an extra ten minutes with my favourite Cornish girl.'

'Mollie will be jealous if she hears you say that.'

'I won't tell if you don't.' Royce winked.

The idea that he made her hot and bothered was flattering but he suspected there was more to it. She'd been oddly quiet when they left Eden earlier apart from inviting him over for a drink later as they parted.

'Do you want to bring the wine glasses out here or is there a chance you'll invite me in?'

'Sorry. I'm a bit flustered. Amy Worthing rang after we got back from the hospital,' she hurried on. 'There's nothing new on Harry but they're fairly certain he's still alive otherwise his body would've been dumped somewhere to be found by now.'

'I guess that's good news.' He raised the bottle again. 'We could celebrate.'

'Come in then.' Rachel's gaze flitted around. 'Why don't you fetch a couple of glasses from the kitchen and I'll . . . clear up the living-room, it's a bit messy.'

He doubted that. She was the neatest person he'd ever met and there'd never been a thing out of place on his previous visits.

'All right if I take my coat off?'

'Of course, I'm sorry. I don't know what's up with me this evening.'

Neither did he but he planned to find out. Royce hitched his heavy black coat over the end of the banister rail and glanced over her shoulder into the living-room. A large cardboard box sat on the coffee table with a bundle of sparkly material, medal ribbons and certificates spilling from it.

'Been having a sort out?'

The fire returned to her cheeks.

'It's a few old skating things. Harry

must've held on to them. They were . . .'

'Hey, you don't have to lie to me. Either tell me it's none of my business or be honest.' His bluntness startled her.

'Do you mind getting the wine glasses first?'

At least she wasn't kicking him out of the door yet. When he returned she'd settled on the sofa although the word settled was an exaggeration. Perched on the edge of the cushion ready to take flight was more accurate. In the short time they'd known each other he'd never seen her so nervous. Royce filled their two glasses.

'Here you go.'

He chose the easy chair by the fireplace and stretched his legs out in front of him.

'How did it feel when you gave up your steady job?' Rachel asked.

Totally not the question he expected her to ask but he tried to explain. One aspect of Rachel he admired, on a rapidly growing list, was her habit of utter concentration.

Her gaze never left him and a tiny furrow creased the space between her eyes. A lock of her glossy hair slipped free but she made no move to brush it away.

'That kind of radical decision isn't for everyone — I get that — but I've no responsibilities beyond myself.' He left the words 'and neither do you' in the air.

'My mum left school at sixteen and married my dad a year later,' Rachel told him. 'She became a hairdresser with the idea she could work as much or as little as she wanted when they started a family.'

Shadows wiped away the remnants of Rachel's smile.

'We mocked her when she insisted on watching every boring history documentary on BBC2 and hauled big, heavy books home from the library. She planned to train as a history teacher when Harry and I were through with school.' Rachel shook her head. 'We laughed at her dreams. How mean was that after she always encouraged Harry and me in everything we wanted to do?'

Royce moved across to sit with her on the sofa.

'Don't be too hard on yourself. Most of us don't see our folks as people with hopes and dreams. We think that's a privilege of the young.' She gazed at him, her eyes glistening with emotion. 'Tell me about your dream,' he added.

She froze.

'You'll laugh . . .'

'Honey, a man wearing a fuzzy orange sweater decorated with a snowman hasn't the right to laugh at anyone.'

Despite everything she couldn't help but smile.

'It is probably your worst jumper ever.'

'Ah but you only think that because you don't know what's hanging in my closet.' He wagged his finger. 'I've got a couple of real crackers to bring out yet . . .' His sandalwood cologne drifted her way. 'It's all wrapped up with ice skating, right?'

'You saw Mollie's face when she started to get the hang of it this afternoon?' She didn't wait for an answer. 'I've forgotten the details of the school plays I acted in and most of my birthday parties are a blur but the moment Dad let go of my hands and I skated myself for the first time — that's etched on my brain even though it's thirty years ago.'

'You're that ancient?'

'Watch what you're saying, old man.'

'Whoa. That's below the belt.'

'Serves you right.' She appreciated the deft way he tossed in a joke to shift a serious conversation back into balance.

'Skating again today brought everything back.' If she told him about meeting Paddy there was no doubt in which direction the conversation would go. She remembered his words: 'Either tell me it's none of my business or be honest.'

'When you and Mollie left I bumped into my old coach.' Rachel gestured to the box. 'It's why I was crawling around in the attic before you came.'

'Mind if I take a look?'

'Help yourself.' Rachel struggled to relax when he checked out several of her medals and prize certificates and then held up a short, red sequinned dress. 'I wore that in my last competition.'

'You won.'

'Yep.' It was the turning point. She beat Sophie Darling and any figure-skating club in the country would've fought to have her join them. 'I couldn't go any further with my skating here and my parents wouldn't let me leave to train out of Cornwall. They claimed it would break up the family but really we couldn't afford it.'

'You resented them.'

'Of course.' They rowed for about a month until her father told her that was the end of it and to concentrate on her school work.

Royce's deep green eyes softened and she panicked, knocking over her glass in her hurry to escape his sympathy. Red wine dripped off the edge of the table on to Anna's cream carpet.

'I'll clean it . . .'

'I'll do it later,' she snapped. 'You asked to hear about my stupid dreams.'

She had never spoken about those dark times. 'Mum packed me off to sleep at my gran's house,' she continued, 'because she'd had enough of my obnoxious behaviour.' Rachel blinked back tears.

'Dad rang the next day to say Mum was sick with the flu but I thought he was using that as an excuse to make me come home and told him where to go.' She paused.

'Later on Harry phoned because Mum was in the Critical Care Unit at Treliske Hospital and Dad had come down with it, too. Gran took me home immediately.'

'How long . . .'

'Mum hung on for about ten days but when she went . . . Dad lost the strength to keep going. We buried them on Christmas Eve.'

'Aw, honey.'

With those two simple words Royce broke through her 20 years of fighting against guilt and grief. He held on to her while racking sobs tore her apart.

'I'm sorry for baiting you about Christmas. No wonder you'd rather forget the whole darned holiday.'

'It brings all the memories flooding back and I can't bear to remember.' The painful words rasped against her sore throat. 'Harry copes better than me and I suppose that makes me feel more of a failure.'

'Maybe he only does on the outside.' Royce shrugged. 'I'm guessing he wouldn't want his army mates seeing him upset. And when he's home? He wouldn't want to spoil Mollie's Christmas but Anna might shore him up to get through the holidays. Ask him when he comes back.'

Rachel shuddered.

'What if I don't get the chance . . .'

'Don't.' He pressed a swift, hard kiss on her mouth. 'Have faith.' Royce picked up the abandoned skating costume.'Remember what else was on Mollie's list?'

'A red party dress.' Wouldn't that be a wonderful use for something special locked away in a box far too long? She met Royce's broad grin and the penny dropped. 'Could you really alter it?'

'Yep, no problem. Sneak me one of Mollie's dresses for a guide to the fit.'

'You never explained where you learned to sew. Did your mum teach you?'

'Hardly.' His rumbling laughter filled the room. Soon he had her laughing along with his story. 'I never wanted to see another dreary grey beggar's costume by the time that was over. It sure killed my crush on Kylie Johnson who only had eyes for the sickeningly handsome class valedictorian and star football player who swaggered through the part of Jean Valjean.'

Her heartbeat raced when he pulled her closer.

'I sure hope you've got a thing for men who can sew, bake and write poetry.' He trailed soft kisses all the way down her neck. 'Put me out of my misery, Rachel.'

With a laugh she tapped his jumper.

'Miserable? While you're wearing a monstrosity like this. Who are you kidding?' Slipping her hands around his waist she snuggled even closer. Logical.

Sensible. Unemotional. Why was she none of those things around this man?

'Let's not over think this,' Royce pleaded. 'I don't know about you but I've done enough of that to last me a lifetime.'

'I can't rush into . . .'

'Not suggesting it, honey.' He cracked a wry smile. 'We're not teenagers and sensible is too ingrained in our DNA to fly off into the sunset.'

'Then what . . .'

'Take it as it comes and be open to whatever comes our way.'

'Sounds reasonable.'

'Good. I'll get the sewing machine and you find a dress Mollie won't miss.' Royce's lingering look made her tingle all over. 'The kid deserves a party dress for forcing you to come knocking on my door to borrow hot chocolate ingredients and marshmallows.'

'She does indeed.'

What Mollie deserved most of all was her father coming home for Christmas but they were running out of time for that miracle.

'Have faith.' Royce read her mind.

In the reflection from the glittering tree lights she recognised confidence and hope in his clear eyes. Rachel wanted to believe.

Change of Heart?

'But Mummy always buys her dress first and then her shoes.' Mollie's exasperation couldn't be clearer. Plainly poor Aunty Rach didn't have a clue how these things were done.

'I know but you specified red, sparkly shoes and they won't be easy to find. We don't want to risk them not having any left in your size. There are still lots of pretty dresses in the shops.' And a particularly nice one taking shape next door if you only knew.

'All right.' Grudging agreement was the best she'd get. 'But I want to see Mummy as well and go ice skating again.'

Don't push your luck, Rachel thought.

'I'll see if I can book another session on Monday. They're bound to be busy over the weekend.'

When Royce tried to persuade her to accept Paddy's offer, even promising to take care of Mollie while she went skating, she'd firmly and politely told him to leave it alone. After he left she couldn't resist digging out her bright red skates from the bottom of the box, custom made to match her last competition dress, and tried them on. The amazing feeling of standing on the podium after winning the south-western championship while Sophie Darling glared from the second place step was the highlight of her life.

Maybe Paddy was right about how good she could've become and maybe he was wrong. Looking back was pointless but she could change the direction of her life going forward.

It was time to hit the shoe shops.

'We'll try Truro first.'

Two excruciating hours later they peered in the window of a tiny shop in one of the back streets of Truro and Mollie jumped up and down with excitement.

'There are my shoes!'

Rachel almost hugged the assistant who measured her niece's feet and promised they had the sparkly red shoes in her size.

Mollie paraded up and down the shop

beaming from ear to ear.

'They're perfect. Now we can go dress shopping.'

'That's enough for one day.' If she wasn't firm the little girl would run over her objections and force her to lie. 'How about lunch at your favourite burger place before we visit your mum?'

'OK, but I want to take her some pretty flowers.'

'We can do that.'

'And presents for the twins.'

The girl was a tough negotiator and Rachel clearly imagined her following in Harry's footsteps. Or becoming an Olympic figure skating champion? She must never project her own dreams on to her niece. Enjoying skating as a fun hobby was one thing. Devoting years to the sport something else entirely.

'Of course.'

'I'm starving. I want lunch first.'

She didn't have the energy to remind the little girl about her manners. One of the prerogatives of being a mere aunt.

'Sounds good to me. Let's go.'

Nothing helped. He played Bing Crosby's 'White Christmas' at full volume, ate freshly baked mince pies for breakfast and wore his favourite twelve days of Christmas jumper before adding an illuminated inflatable angel to his front garden display. Even though the dress he altered for Mollie looked amazing, Royce couldn't slough off his grey mood.

He turned the sealed red envelope over and over as if he could divine what it said through the thick paper. His mother's impeccable handwriting was unmistakeable but why would she send what looked suspiciously like a Christmas card? They didn't 'do' Christmas.

Since his father's retirement his parents always travelled over the holiday season and purposely chose remote locations where they wouldn't be forced into joining any celebrations. The last he heard they'd booked to do a tour of Peru and the ancient Inca empire.

The doorbell rang and Royce threw

the card back on the table.

'I hope we're not disturbing you.' Rachel gave him a quizzical look and he swiftly readjusted his expression into something resembling a smile.

'We found my shoes and they're perfect.' Mollie waved around a shopping bag. 'Aunty Rach says you might have a surprise for me.' She tried to peek around him. 'I love surprises.'

'I'm sorry. I should've rung first but . . .'

'No, it's fine. Come on in.'

Mollie raced past them in a blur of excitement.

'Are you all right?' Rachel touched his arm.

'I got a Christmas card from my folks, OK?'

'I thought they didn't . . .'

'They don't.'

'What did they say?' Rachel persisted.

'How do I know? I haven't opened it yet and yeah that's dumb.'

'I can't see anything different,' Mollie complained. 'Where's the surprise?'

135

'You'll see.' Royce held out his hands and the little girl quickly grabbed one. For a moment he didn't think Mollie would play along but when he dredged up a brighter smile slipped her small, warm hand into his. 'When we get in the living-room I want you to close your eyes. No peeking.'

He steered them around the sofa.

'You can open them now.'

'Oh, wow! Is that for me? It's awesome. It's the sparkliest dress ever.' Mollie's joy lifted his spirits and behind the little girl's back Rachel beamed at him.

'Why don't you try it on while I fix our daily dose of hot chocolate? And make sure you ask Aunty Rach to tell you the story behind this dress.'

'It's got a story?'

'It sure has.'

Rachel didn't look too thrilled but he left them alone and disappeared into the kitchen purposely taking his time before returning with a tray of hot drinks and cookies.

'Look, Mr Roy.' Mollie twirled around.

136

'I'm the Christmas Fairy.'

He pretended to size her up.

'It's a shame you're too big to stick on top of my Christmas tree.'

'You're silly. You can't use real people.'

'That's right,' Rachel teased. 'Mollie, you need to change your dress so you don't spill hot chocolate over it.'

'But I want to wear it.' Tears welled up in her big, blue eyes.

'Remember it's a special dress and you need to take care of it.' Royce watched her mull over his words.

'I know.' Mollie let out a heavy sigh. 'It's just so pretty.' She smoothed her hands over the rich red silk. 'Can I keep on my shoes? Please.'

He suppressed a smile. Rachel's mouth twitched and if he dared to look directly at her they'd both laugh.

'Deal.'

Mollie disappeared to the bathroom and Rachel instantly harangued him about opening his parents' Christmas card.

'It's like ripping off a plaster or yanking out a loose tooth.'

'Did we need the dental analogy?'

'Stop prevaricating.'

Before he could joke about her using big words she grabbed the envelope and thrust it at him.

'Fine.' He pulled out the card. 'I expect it says 'Merry Christmas. Bah Humbug!''

'For heaven's sake — I thought I was stubborn.' Rachel snatched it away and stared at the front, turning pale. Tentatively she opened up the card and read the inside.

'I'm sorry.' All her remaining colour seeped away. 'It's time I took Mollie home. We've had a long day and we're both tired.'

'It doesn't bother me that you read it.'

'You might . . .'

'Babe, it's OK.' Royce brushed a quick kiss over her cheek.

'Is my hot chocolate cool enough to drink?' Mollie raced back in and plonked down on the sofa.

'It should be about perfect. There's something I need from the kitchen but

I'll be right back.' He prised the card away from Rachel and made his escape.

The front of the card with its greeting to 'A Dear Son at Christmas' and the sentimental verse inside affected him deeply but reading his mother's hand-written note forced him to bite back tears.

Words of Love

They had the red party dress and sparkly shoes so Rachel crossed off number six on Mollie's list. Along with the fact they hadn't received any bad news about Harry she should consider this a satisfying day but couldn't get Royce out of her mind.

After he rejoined them he did his best to play along with Mollie's bubbling enthusiasm for all things Christmas, and especially her 'new' dress, but his heart wasn't in it.

She felt awful leaving him alone next door with his sadness but couldn't abandon Mollie to check on him. If she rang him up what could she say? Rachel wandered over to look out of the window and smiled.

Thanks to Royce and Mollie she admired the twinkling lights along Poltair Road without considering it tacky and tasteless. Her parents always loved Christmas and she should embrace their legacy. Buying a Christmas jumper might be going too far but a red blouse might not reach too far out of her comfort zone.

Rachel blinked to make sure she wasn't seeing things. Royce's house sat in complete darkness. All of a sudden she heard voices outside getting closer and picked out the strains of 'Away in a Manger'.

Number seven. Go carol singing.

Mollie hadn't been asleep very long and didn't have school tomorrow so what did it matter if she was tired in the morning?

'Wake up, sweetheart. There are carol singers outside.' She roused her niece and encouraged her to put on her cute elf slippers and warm red dressing gown.

'Really?'

'Yes, really. Hurry up or we'll miss them.'

They bundled out of the door and spotted a small crowd of their neighbours gathered in a circle around a group of carol singers dressed in Dickensian era outfits and swinging old-fashioned lanterns. The only thing needed to make it absolutely perfect was a soft layer of snow on the ground but with the recent mild temperatures that wasn't likely.

'We need to tell Mr Roy to come out.' Mollie pleaded. 'He loves Christmas carols.'

'I don't think he's home because there aren't any lights on.'

'His lights must be broken. I'm going to knock on his door.' She raced off before Rachel could stop her. Even after pressing the bell three times with no answer her stubborn niece refused to leave. 'Mr Roy, it's Mollie. Hurry up.'

'What's up, kiddo?' Royce peeked out around the door. No white, bright smile tonight.

'Didn't you hear the carol singers? You've got to come.' Mollie grabbed his hand. 'Come on or we'll miss it.'

'I'm not . . .'

'But it's on my list. You have to.'

'If you're busy don't worry.' Rachel tried to give him a way out.

'Aunty Rach! Don't you want Mr Roy

to come?'

'Of course I do, but . . .'

'Then that's that,' Mollie declared.

'Yeah, that's that, Ms Rachel.' Royce's smooth, amused drawl sounded more normal. Maybe her niece had the right idea. 'I'll get my coat.'

'You need one of your funny jumpers and you forgot to put your lights on. Your house looks unhappy.'

'Oops, sorry.' He disappeared for a few seconds and next thing the outside of number 19 blazed with colour. 'Satisfied?' The sight of his teasing smile lifted Rachel's spirits. 'Does this meet your fashion standards, Miss Mollie?'

He strutted outside to join them, spinning around to show off his gaudy jumper.

'If they sing 'Jingle Bells' I can dance along.' The string of silver bells stretched across his broad chest jangled in the clear, night air and Mollie burst into giggles.

A woman could easily fall in love with this wonderful man. The thought sent

Rachel into a panic until Royce latched on to her gaze. All of a sudden the idea wasn't as scary any more.

Whoa, what happened there? He just proved the quotes were spot on when it came to a person's eyes being the window to the soul. Only dumb people like him hadn't seen what everyone from Cicero to the Bible and William Shakespeare realised centuries ago. Without speaking the words out loud he'd told her he loved her and she said it right back at him.

'Hurry up or we'll miss it,' Mollie complained. 'You and Aunty Rach are being weird.'

No time to muse about the meaning of life and love around a six-year-old. He draped his arm around Rachel's shoulder and lowered his voice.

'Come on, weird Aunty Rach. Don't worry — we'll make up for this later.' Despite the chill in the air a bloom of heat radiated from her pale skin.

'Uh, the grass is wet,' Mollie complained. 'I'll spoil my elf slippers.'

'Let me carry you.' Royce swept the

little girl up in his arms.

'Woo hoo, Rachel.'

He recognised the blonde waving across at them.

'That's Hannah's mummy,' Mollie squealed. 'I want to tell them all about my sparkly shoes and dress.'

He sensed Rachel's reluctance.

'Why don't we hang on here, kiddo? You can see your friends later.' The choir began to sing 'O Little Town of Bethlehem' and Mollie was quickly distracted. His hearty baritone was loud and tuneful enough to earn him one of Rachel's knowing smiles.

After the carol finished he noticed a lot of people pointing and whispering in their direction but wasn't vain enough to believe his singing was the cause.

All of a sudden it clicked and his brain raced, working overtime to come up with an inconspicuous way to get all of them, but Mollie in particular, out of there. Many people knew, or knew of, Rachel and her family.

Harry's disappearance wasn't a secret

any longer and any minute now they'd be swamped by well-wishers and curiosity seekers.

The choir leader announced that during their final carol, 'We Wish You a Merry Christmas', they'd pass around a collecting tin in aid of a local homeless charity.

'I'm pretty sure today is a double hot chocolate day,' Royce suggested and Rachel's eyes flared with annoyance until she glanced around and caught on to his meaning.

'It is indeed. I vote for extra marshmallows.'

Mollie stared between them both as though she couldn't believe her luck.

'Off we go.' He stuffed a wad of money in the nearest collecting tin. 'We'll drink it in your house tonight then you'll be close to your bed when you get sleepy.'

'I'm too excited to sleep. There are only a few more sleeps before my daddy comes home and Mummy has our babies.'

If Rachel thought she could keep the

news about Harry from this smart little girl very much longer she was fooling herself. If they didn't tell her, someone else would.

★ ★ ★

'She barely stirred when I tucked her in.' Rachel sunk down on the sofa next to Royce with a heavy sigh. 'You think I'm stubborn not to tell her.'

'Not stubborn. Maybe a tad on the scared side and I don't blame you.'

'How do I tell Mollie her father is missing and could be dead?'

'Separate the two things.' He leaned forward. 'Start by explaining he got lost on patrol and hasn't found his way back yet but lots of people are looking for him.'

'But what if . . .'

''What if' will hopefully never happen. Deal with it then if you're forced to.'

'Anna made me swear not to say a word to Mollie.'

He looked thoughtful.

'She's in a bubble at the hospital and focused on her babies.'

'Are you suggesting she doesn't care about Mollie or Harry?' Rachel's outrage erupted but disappeared in the shadow of his gentle smile. 'Sorry. I know you didn't mean that . . . you're being sensible . . . I'm not.'

'It's simpler for me. I'm a step removed.'

The only possible decision to make crystallised in her mind. She'd break the news to Mollie in the morning and inform Anna afterwards. If her sister-in-law ranted and raved at her so be it.

'It'll be OK.'

She snuggled into Royce's arms and decided that if she wrapped him in a big red bow he'd be the best Christmas present she could ever wish for. Rachel savoured the moment until she glanced over to the mantelpiece where they'd arranged all of the cards from Mollie's school friends. She could've kicked herself.

'Hey, sweetheart, don't beat up on

148

yourself — it's not a matter of life or death.' Rachel searched his open gaze for any clue that he was simply trying to make her feel better. 'I'm not complicated and I'm not hiding anything from you.' Royce brushed a soft kiss over her mouth. 'Yeah, I was upset earlier but now I'm more . . . puzzled.'

'Out of nowhere your mum leaves your dad after forty-five years of marriage and you're puzzled?'

He tried to explain his mother's lifelong habit of quietly agreeing with her stern husband, never giving any sign that she found his rigid principles abhorrent.

'She never said a word when he chastised me for spending my pocket money on Christmas cards for my class at school. I was eight and I didn't want the other kids to mock me.' Royce rested his hands on his knees.

'Hallowe'en was the worst. My father called it a pagan holiday used as an excuse to encourage children to stuff themselves with teeth-rotting candy.' He struggled to smile. 'Typical spoilsport dentist.'

'Have you rung your mother?'

'And say what? That it's a bit late now to make amends but have a nice life?'

Rachel longed to plead with him to be generous. Bitterness corroded a person. Resentment over her parents' early deaths ate away her fundamentally loving nature and only now, at nearly forty, did she appreciate what a fool she'd been.

Over the years Harry tried to make her see reason but she blocked him and anyone else who attempted to burrow under the hard surface she presented to the world. But this wonderful man ignored every obstacle she placed in his way until she'd no defences left.

'I'm dumb, aren't I?' The rhetorical question made them both smile. 'We can't make other people's choices for them.' He dragged the crumpled up Christmas card from his jeans pocket and smoothed it out. 'That took guts to send because she probably assumed I'd throw it in the trash.'

'You're better than that.'

Royce brushed at his eyes with the back of one hand.

'Am I?'

'Yes. If you weren't I wouldn't love you.'

'Hey, do you know what you . . .'

'Of course I know what I said. I don't make a habit of telling men I love them without meaning it.' Her face and neck burned. 'Actually, I've never . . .'

'Neither have I, sweetheart.' Royce blushed. 'Unless you're gonna call me out because I pledged my love to Sara Beth Wingate when I was five years old. My only excuse is that she offered me a piece of chocolate caramel fudge and I'd never tasted it before.'

'You are so cheap. Load you up with sugar and you're anyone's.'

'Not any longer.' He caressed her hair, playing with the shaggy ends. 'I love it's a little messier these days. Like our lives.'

'But . . .'

'Shush.' Royce's searing gaze rested on her and he drew them into a heart-stopping kiss. 'Yeah, better than hot chocolate.'

'Oh, my, he really does love me.'

'Yeah, I really do.'

Before she could kiss him again Rachel's phone vibrated and the liaison officer's number flashed up on the screen. Her hands trembled as she answered the call, only vaguely aware of Royce's comforting arm around her shoulder as she struggled to register Amy's words.

A Festive Feast

'Why don't you come and spend Christmas here with me, Mom?' The offer tumbled out into silence. 'There's someone I'd like you to meet.'

'A girl?'

'A woman,' Royce gently corrected her. 'She's special.'

'I'm not sure I'd be very good company.'

This hadn't been the easiest conversation on either side.

'I suppose you've gone overboard on Christmas as usual.' His mother's critical attitude returned and he struggled to justify Rachel's faith in his ability to rise above past resentments.

'Yeah, I sure have. It makes me happy and doesn't harm anyone else.'

'I'm sorry, son. I didn't mean . . .'

'Hey, don't fret. It'll take us a while but we'll do OK.' He thought he'd better ask about his father. 'Have you moved out of the house?'

'Yes, I'm in a hotel at the moment but I told your dad I'll move out properly when he gets back from Peru and we've got the time to divide everything up.

'At least I don't have to be bored out of my mind trailing around more dusty old ruins.' She chuckled. 'Your father is one himself so he should fit right in.'

Royce laughed with her and it struck him they'd rarely shared a joke before.

'If you stay there in Nashville you'll be on your own. Come over here for a week or so and we'll enjoy a typical English Christmas together.'

'Your young lady might not appreciate me turning up out of the blue.'

'I've told Rachel about you ... and what's going on with dad. She'd be pleased to meet you.'

'Hasn't she invited you to join her family for the holidays?'

Royce explained the situation and by the time they ended the call she'd agreed to check on available flights. He saw Rachel's smart, black Peugeot parked outside the house which meant they hadn't left to visit Anna yet.

Mollie opened the door and beamed.

'Did you know my daddy was playing hide and seek and no-one could find him because he's the cleverest person in the world?'

'Well . . .'

'Now someone says they've found him but the people playing the game have to pay a forfeit,' she babbled on. 'When I play with my friends we do things like tell a joke or hop on one leg for a forfeit but I s'pose it's different for grown-ups.'

'Are you free to come with us to the hospital?' Rachel pleaded.

'You've got to help with my list.' Despite her abbreviated night's sleep Mollie's battery was fully recharged. 'I need four more things and we still haven't seen Father Christmas and petted a reindeer.'

'I'm sure I can come up with a few ideas. We could work on your list while Aunty Rach has a chat with your mom and then you can go see her. How about we ride in my car today?' Royce grinned.

'It's got reindeer ears on the roof and a bright red nose on the front.' A faint trace of humour helped soften Rachel's strained face.

'Oh, yes please!'

'Hurry up and get ready then we'll go,' Rachel urged. 'Parking will be a nightmare.'

'Don't worry, kiddo, Rudolph always tracks down a good spot for the sleigh.'

'You're funny.' Mollie giggled and ran off upstairs.

'We don't have long,' Royce warned. 'Tell me what's going on.'

'I don't know what to think.' She reiterated Amy Worthing's phone call word for word.

The same shepherd who first claimed to see Harry limping into a cave approached the authorities again and demanded a reward before he gave them more information.

He insisted a local family who lived further up in the mountains took Harry home with them and were helping him recover from his injuries.

'Amy says there are inconsistencies in his story. If they send out a full search team it might put his fellow soldiers' lives at risk because there's a strong possibility it's a set up and they'll be ambushed.'

'But they can't ignore it.' Royce's protest touched her.

'They're not, but they need to check it out more first. I'm as anxious as anyone but there's nothing we can do.'

He wrapped her in a tight hug but let go when he heard the little girl's footsteps on the stairs.

She longed to hold on to Royce's comforting touch but succumbed to the inevitable.

'Is your Rudolph car ready, Mr Roy?' Mollie hopped into the room, grinning.

'Come on, ladies.'

Why wasn't she surprised when Royce tuned his radio on a station playing Christmas music and turned the drive to Truro into a joy-filled sing-along?

'We're very early.' Rachel noticed as they drove into the car park. 'Visiting hours don't start until half past two.'

'Nobody's had any lunch, right?'

'No, but I thought we could grab a quick sandwich in the café.'

'Don't want a sandwich.' Mollie tugged at her seat belt. 'I want to see my Mummy.'

'You will, sweetie,' Royce promised. 'But your mom is eating her lunch now and I'm pretty sure she'll need a nap before visiting time.' He pointed to a big red cardboard box on the back seat. 'I packed a special reindeer food picnic for us to eat in the car.'

'Oh, wow!'

'Have you any idea how much you'll end up paying to park?' Rachel warned. His gentle smile broadened and he leaned over to brush a soft kiss on her cheek.

'She's happy, OK?' Royce shrugged. 'Hop in the back seat with Mollie and pass me the box. I'll fix our picnic.'

She gave in because it was easier, plus by now she was almost as curious as her niece.

'We've got Rudolph Rolls and Red

158

Nose balls.' He pulled out sausage rolls with attached pastry ears and fresh cherry tomatoes. 'This is reindeer food. It's their favourite thing.' Royce handed them individual bags with a mixture of nuts and dried fruit.

'And there's Santa Squash to drink.' He poured the lurid red drink into Christmassy paper cups. 'If you eat all that I've got a special treat for dessert.'

'Yummy.' Mollie happily munched away.

With the radio playing carols in the background they didn't talk much until there were only a few crumbs left of lunch.

Royce peered dramatically into the picnic box. He pulled out three small boxes beautifully wrapped in gold paper with flashy red bows and passed the first to Mollie.

'Oh.' Mollie's eyes widened. 'It says my name and it's all sparkly.'

Rachel opened her own box and stared at the beautiful cupcake with her name picked out in gold sprinkles.

For a moment she was overcome by his thoughtfulness.

'It's a ginger cake with honey butter cream frosting.'

'It's beautiful.' She met his gaze and a deep flush crept up his neck while her own cheeks burned.

'This one is for Anna and the babies.' Royce held up a fourth box.

'They're far too pretty to eat.' She admired the miniature work of art. There seemed no end to this amazing man's talents.

'No, they're not,' Mollie mumbled through a mouthful of cupcake.

'The munchkin's right.' He tipped her a mischievous wink and ate half of his treat in one gigantic bite.

'Fine. If you both insist.' Rachel ploughed into the soft, sweet delicacy and thought she'd died and gone to heaven. 'Oh, goodness — that rivals any French bakery.'

'I'm honoured.' Royce bowed his head. 'I know you Europeans are fussy about your cakes.'

'Oh, stop it. I'm trying to pay you a compliment. Take it.'

'I will, sweetheart, I will.' Royce's deep, rich drawl seeped into her and she nearly melted into the seat. 'Let's go on in. I'll find a quiet spot to sit and work with Mollie on her Christmas wish list. Send a text when you're ready for us to come up.'

That brought Rachel back to reality. She shouldn't laugh and joke when her poor brother was being held, probably against his will, in a remote part of Afghanistan.

'You're keeping up your end of the deal. Mollie's happy. Anna's taken care of. That's all Harry expects.'

'Thanks for always understanding.'

'The same back at you.'

I truly love this man, Rachel thought.

Full of Surprises

'Ok, number nine is to make Christmas presents for your mom and dad and the babies. Number ten is to see a pantomime.' Royce chuckled. 'That'll be a first for me, kiddo. We don't have them in America.'

'My mummy and daddy took me to see 'Puss in Boots' last Christmas. There's lots of singing and dancing and people being silly. It's fun,' Mollie explained. 'What else?'

He needed to choose the right words.

'You get lots of new toys for Christmas don't you?'

'Yes.' She sounded suspicious.

'And your bedroom is pretty full of toys already, right?' Mollie frowned in a very Rachel-like way. He suddenly hit on how to connect this with Harry.

'Where your daddy is working a lot of the moms and dads don't have any spare money to buy toys for their children. We could send them the ones you don't play with any longer.'

'I s'pose so.' The idea hadn't quite caught her imagination.

'I could take a picture of you with all the toys you pick out then you can show Daddy when he comes home. He'll be so proud of you. It's good to do things for other people who aren't as lucky as we are.'

Was that too hard for a six-year-old to understand?

'OK. Mummy says I must try not to be sad about my daddy not being here because he helps people and that's important.'

A rush of emotion swept through Royce.

'Your mom is right and you're a very brave girl.'

'How many days do we have left now?' Mollie sighed.

'That's number eleven.' He tried to come up with something easy to wrap up the list but his phone buzzed with an incoming text. 'We can go see your mom now,' he told Mollie.

'But we haven't finished.'

'How about we have a party for some of your friends?' Rachel would kill him. 'You can all wear your party dresses and we'll bake cookies and make Christmas decorations for them to take home.'

'That's awesome.' She flung her arms around his neck and almost squeezed the breath out of him.

If he didn't put some limits on this, Mollie would invite everyone she knew.

'I think six friends is enough or we won't have enough room.'

'Cool. I want Sophie and Alison and . . .' She nibbled on her thumb, deep in concentration.

'Let's go see your mom now and decide who to invite later. We've got to work out with Aunty Rach what day is best for the party.' Assuming we're allowed to have one, he added silently.

'OK.' Mollie jumped up and dragged at his hand. 'Come on.'

The Trewarren women were always ordering him around but funnily enough he loved it.

* * *

Rachel snuggled into his arms, happy to give Anna and Mollie time alone together.

'Did you get the list finished?' Did he seem sheepish or was that her overactive imagination? 'What outrageous ideas did you come up with now?'

'Outrageous? You're hard on me.'

'I simply see right through you. Spit it out.'

He trotted out numbers nine, ten and eleven on Mollie's list.

'I assume you'll supervise present making? I wouldn't know where to start.'

'No problem. I help an at-risk kids' group in St Austell and we did a few easy projects with them a few weeks ago . . .' Royce stared. 'What?'

'You never stop surprising me.'

He gave a sideways smile.

'I guess that's a good thing? Who wants to be bored by someone they . . . love?'

'It's all right to use the L word,' Rachel whispered. 'I've concluded it's no respecter of time. A few weeks, months, years . . . what does it matter?'

'Doesn't in the least to me, sweetheart.' Brushing back a strand of hair, he kissed her forehead.

'I haven't been to a pantomime in years but Mollie will love that. The unwanted toy thing is a brilliant idea. She's a good kid.'

'She sure is.'

'Before we get interrupted again you'd better break the bad news to me about number twelve on Mollie's list.'

'What makes you . . . it's a party.'

'A party?'

'I've laid down the rules.' Before she had a chance to protest Royce rattled off the details. 'You pick the day and time.'

'How generous of you.' Seven hyperactive little girls excited about Christmas and loaded with sugary treats. Rachel couldn't imagine why she hadn't come up with the idea herself. 'Let's get it over with as soon as possible. How about Saturday afternoon if that works for her friends?'

'Um, that's a bit tricky. Don't freak out before I finish.' The combination of his accent and the garbled speed with which he raced through the story meant she only caught about two-thirds of his appalling idea. Two-thirds was enough.

'No. Definitely not. I told Mollie Holly Jolly Christmas Land wasn't an option.'

'But it's the only place in Cornwall to meet both Father Christmas and pet a live reindeer.' He grabbed her hands.

'I'd offer to take Mollie on my own but we're treating the at-risk children's group to an afternoon there on Saturday and I'm one of the chaperones. It won't be a problem if you and Mollie tag along.' He caressed her cheek.

'It's only for a couple of hours.'

'Did you con your dental patients into thinking their treatment wouldn't hurt the same devious way?'

'I'm offended.' The sparkle in his bright green eyes belied his words.

'Good.'

'Help me out here, Rachel. Why is this such a sticking point?'

Afraid of breaking down if she told him the complete truth Rachel tried to glance away but he didn't let her.

'It was our family tradition to go there when we got out of school for the Christmas holidays. OK?'

Wonderful memories of visiting the theme park with her parents and Harry filled her head. It was the highlight of the holidays and the last place they went as a family before tragedy ripped them apart.

'It's meant for younger children, really, but we begged to go one more year and of course our parents gave in. This was right when we were having the fuss about my ice skating. Mum had a cold coming on . . .'

'The start of the flu?'

She nodded through tears.

'After twenty-one years it shouldn't still hurt this much.'

Royce tightened his arms around her and she cried until there were no tears left.

'If Harry and I hadn't . . .'

'Stop. Your folks loved you and did

everything they could to make you happy. A slight cold wasn't going to stop your mom. Good parents aren't made that way.' Rachel nodded as Royce suddenly sat back.

'We've been so caught up in everything,' he suddenly added, 'I forgot to ask how Anna's doing.'

Rachel explained how it had wrung her out to see her poor sister-in-law struggling to be brave. The doctor had warned they couldn't delay Anna going into labour much longer so the clock was ticking for Harry to make it back home for the twins' birth.

'I'm guessing you've heard nothing more from the army?'

'No.' She was thankful Royce simply nodded without making any promises.

'I talked to my mom,' he told her. 'On Friday she's off to see her sister in Charlotte, North Carolina for the first time in ages. She'll fly out of there on Saturday and arrive in London the next morning.

'Her train gets here around mid-afternoon on Sunday. I'm pretty sure she'll be too tired for the pantomime but I bought an extra ticket.'

'We have tickets?'

'Yeah, to see 'Sleeping Beauty' at the St Mervyn village hall. Is that OK?'

'Aunty Rach, look at this.' Mollie raced in, followed by a smiling young nurse. 'I've got a picture of our babies. They took it through Mummy's tummy. That's my brother, Noel Andrew Trewarren,' she pointed to one of the blurry shapes, 'and that,' her stubby finger jabbed the other wriggling baby, 'is my sister, Holly Jane Trewarren.'

'That's wonderful.' Anna had sworn they didn't want to find out the sex of the babies before they were born but obviously something made her change her mind. Perhaps she needed a boost, something concrete to hold on to.

'We finished our list. Did you see it?'

'I did and it's brilliant.'

'But we haven't petted a reindeer yet and you . . .'

'Mr Roy came up with a great idea to solve that problem.' She couldn't hold out any longer. 'Father Christmas and some of his reindeer are at Holly Jolly Christmas Land . . .'

'You said . . .'

'I changed my mind.' Rachel plastered on her brightest smile.

'You're the best.'

If she hadn't been sitting down Mollie's hug would've knocked her off her feet.

'We'll go on Saturday afternoon.'

'I'm coming, too,' Royce said and explained about the group of children they'd be with. Mollie's sympathetic response touched Rachel. Harry and Anna should be proud of their kind-hearted daughter.

'It must be hot chocolate time.' Mollie beamed. 'With extra, extra, extra marshmallows.'

If any little girl deserved her Christmas wishes to come true it was her sweet niece.

A Lifetime Together?

If he hadn't spent a couple of hours helping Mollie to sort through her toys this morning Royce would have climbed up the nearest wall. Every time the dancing reindeer in his living-room performed and his Christmas tree lights flashed he wondered what his mother would think of it all.

Just because she'd separated from his father didn't mean it would be easy to leave behind 40 years of antagonism when it came to the holidays.

Interestingly enough, on the phone she confessed to loving everything about Christmas as a child until she met Stuart Carver at university. Dazzled by his brilliant intellect she changed her way of thinking to match his and blocked everything else out.

One thing puzzled Royce. When he asked how his father reacted to her request for a separation she went very quiet and refused to talk about it. Maybe things weren't as cut and dried as she made out.

Tracking down the craft supplies they needed would help him stay busy. He couldn't offer to take Rachel and Mollie on his shopping trip because they'd gone ice skating again. When he asked whether she'd given any more thought to her old coach's offer Rachel shut him down. Maybe she didn't know him as well as she thought if she believed he'd give up that easily.

For now he'd concentrate on searching for lollipop sticks. After doing some research he discovered that was the British name for popsicle sticks. The ubiquitous wood sticks were used in so many kids' crafts in the States the company would never go out of business.

Royce rifled through his wardrobe for a jumper to wear for his shopping trip. His hand hovered over a plain navy one. Stupid. He went with one of his old favourites — the elf one he loaned to Rachel.

His mother must take him as he was or not at all.

Absentmindedly he answered his mobile while searching the cluttered kitchen table for his car keys.

'Dad?' The line was terrible. 'What's that? You've cut short your trip to Peru and you're back in Nashville but Mom's not there?' He must be careful how much he said. If she wanted his father to know her exact whereabouts she'd have left a note.

'But you knew she'd moved out so why are you surprised? I'm sure she's fine.' Royce held the phone away from his ear. 'We've spoken, OK?' His father's rant continued for several minutes until he ran out of steam.

'You know where she is.' There wasn't a single word about loving and missing his wife, which shouldn't be unexpected because Royce had never seen any sign of tenderness or affection between his parents. 'But you won't tell me.'

For a moment he thought they'd been cut off but it was emotion rather than a bad connection causing his father's voice to crack.

'I don't blame you, son.' That made a change. 'I get we've had our ups and downs.' Understatement of the year. 'I've not been a good father. I suppose I didn't know how. Your grandfather Carver was a hard man.'

For the first time ever Royce experienced a twinge of pity for the man who made his childhood a misery.

'Did Marilyn tell you I bullied her?'

'Not in so many words.'

'Well, I did.' The admission stunned Royce. 'And you.'

He wondered where this revelation came from but couldn't decide how to phrase the question without his lingering bitterness poisoning the conversation.

'I need to talk to you both in person.' Stuart exhaled a heavy sigh. 'I don't suppose either of you want to see me and I don't expect us to start playing happy families anytime soon but if you'll hear me out and allow me to apologise I'd appreciate it.'

Royce was flabbergasted. 'Could you pass my message on to your mother?'

'Yeah, I guess.' He needed to give his father something. 'I'll give you a call back when I've spoken to her and um . . . as for me, how about we have a chat when I return to Nashville?'

'Thanks, son.'

He held on to the phone long after his father hung up. Later he'd call his mom but right now he desperately needed to talk to Rachel. He could join them at the skating rink for a short while then leave to do his shopping. On the way out of the door he grabbed the matching elf hat. Anything to make Mollie smile.

★ ★ ★

Even in a sea of festive wear Rachel spotted Royce. There weren't any other six-foot-four-inch elves around to compete with his bright green and red jumper, pointy cap and jangling bells.

'Yoohoo, Mr Roy.' Mollie's frantic waving knocked her niece off balance and her feet slipped out from under her. She crashed down on the ice and burst out laughing. It reminded Rachel of the millions of times she ended up on her backside and picked herself up to keep skating. Considering it was only her second time Mollie was doing an amazing job and they'd already booked a third lesson on Sunday morning.

'Hi, girls.' He leaned over the rail. 'How's it going?'

'This is so much fun. I wish you could join us.'

'Yeah, so do I. When you're finished how about I treat us all to a snack?'

Something was up because his smile stopped at the corners of his mouth.

'You haven't heard anything new about Harry?' Rachel's heart thumped.

'No, honey.' Royce's reassurance seeped in. 'I need your take on something, that's all.'

'Give us ten minutes and we'll meet you in the café.' She watched him stroll off and wondered again how he carried off the gaudy jumper/hat combination without looking ridiculous? People smiled and pointed as he walked by but always in an amiable way and Royce happily high-fived a couple of laughing kids.

'I like Mr Roy, he's fun.' Mollie's proclamation made her smile. 'You like him too, don't you? My mummy says you like him a lot.'

Oh, does she, Rachel thought.

'If you married Mr Roy, would you stay here? I'd like that.'

Married? Where did that come from? Anna, the eternal matchmaker?

'He's a good friend, that's all.'

'But he loves you and you love him. I heard you.'

Rachel's face and neck flamed.

'You shouldn't listen at doors. Let's hurry up and return our skates. We won't talk about this to Mr Roy, OK?'

He'd be mortified and assume she was angling for a proposal. No, you're the one who's mortified, she told herself. Royce would laugh, fall very quiet then give her a dark, searching stare.

She'd receive the clear message he didn't consider the idea at all bizarre. In the past Rachel never pictured herself getting married and, unlike so many little girls, hadn't made up stories around her ideal wedding.

What exactly did she mean when she told Royce she loved him a few days ago? Were these feelings enough to consider committing to a lifetime together?

'It's our secret,' Mollie whispered. 'I won't tell him you want to get married.'

Not precisely what she meant to imply but if it kept her niece's mouth shut that would do for now.

★ ★ ★

'Sit by me?' Royce patted the empty chair next to him. 'I've got a clear line of vision over here to keep an eye on Mollie.' She'd spotted a couple of girls from her class sitting with their mothers in the café and run over to join them.

Royce almost forgot where they were and kissed her, something she wouldn't appreciate in front of prying eyes.

'I hate to spoil the moment,' she

glanced over her shoulder, 'but our chaperone won't be gone long and you wanted to talk.'

'Need. Not want.' Worry shaded her clear grey eyes. 'Hey, it's nothing to do with us . . . well . . . it is — but not us as a couple.' The touch of amusement curving the edges of her mouth stopped him wittering on. Royce launched into what was rapidly becoming the soap-opera saga of his parents.

'That's where things stand.' He shoved his fingers through his hair dislodging the elf hat. 'I guess I'll call Mom when I'm back at the house and take it from there. I know it's their marriage to sort out but . . . seeing a different side to them both is confusing me.'

'All you can do is be there for them both but make it clear you aren't taking sides.'

'I'm not a tightrope artist.' He struggled to crack a joke.

'A couple?' Rachel's breathless voice was barely audible. 'You called us a couple.'

'Is that a problem?'

'I . . . don't think so.'

'But?'

'Mr Roy.' Mollie tugged on his arm. 'Did Aunty Rach tell you all my friends can come to my party?'

'Yeah, that's great.' He checked the time. 'I'm afraid I need to hurry up and go while the shops are still open.'

'I want to come, too.'

'Why don't we all go?' Rachel suggested.

Another important conversation shifted to the back burner. Soon he'd be juggling them like flaming torches.

The Best News

Rachel's head throbbed from the lingering effect of partying with seven excited little girls.

She and Royce had barely survived the last three hours and Rachel kissed Mollie goodnight more enthusiastically than usual when she made little more than a token protest at bedtime. She fell asleep still wearing her party outfit and Rachel eased off the red sparkly shoes before tucking her niece under the covers.

Finally, she returned to the living-room and sank into the chair opposite Royce.

'That was a neat idea to take photos of the girls all dressed up and the pictures looked great in the frames they made. I'd never have thought to use lollipop sticks.' His obvious embarrassment touched her. 'I'm sure we'll find glitter in every corner of this house for weeks.'

The conversation ebbed away.

'You up for revisiting the 'couple' conversation?' Royce mused.

At work she never hesitated to tackle difficult issues, whether it was a tricky software glitch or a personnel problem but now she'd happily turn into an ostrich and bury her head in the sand.

'I've never been to Paris,' Royce suddenly said. A rush of heat zoomed up her neck. This was her signal to respond with an invitation, or not. She should be pleased he wasn't steering them into a commitment they weren't ready for but it irked her to have the choice placed firmly in her lap.

But he loves you and you love him, she reminded herself.

'Tell me what you want, Rachel.'

'It's not that simple.' She jumped up from the sofa. Pacing around the room she avoided the space around him because she didn't trust herself. For two pins she'd behave in a very un-Rachel like way and throw herself at him.

'Did I say it was?' He made a swift move to stand in front of her, giving her no chance to move away before wrapping her in a tight hug. Hints of warm apple cider and cinnamon still clung to him and Rachel wriggled closer.

'Is that better?' He trailed kisses up her neck until he reached her mouth. 'If you want to simply be friends tell me now.'

'Would you be happy with that?' Rachel scoffed before bursting out laughing. 'Wow — even for me that's a stupid question.'

'Yeah, pretty much, and I'm sure it's not enough for you, either.'

'No.'

'Don't panic. We've got a lot going on right now. Let's be loving friends, a couple or whatever we want. Definitions aren't important.' He stroked her cheek. 'When things are more settled we'll work out where we go next.' Royce cleared his throat. 'I hope it'll be together in some way.'

'Me, too.' She worked her fingers through his tousled hair. 'We've talked enough for one day.'

'We sure have.'

Royce's eyes gleamed.

★ ★ ★

As streaks of pink and gold crept into the sky Rachel wrapped her hands around her tea mug to stay warm and stared out across the garden wall.

She always laughed at her mother who loved nothing better than getting out of bed early to watch the sun rise. Once she tried it she became hooked, too.

Perhaps it was all wrapped up with being in Cornwall again but her parents felt more real these days, unlike the ghostly figures they'd become with the passing years. She often talked to them and asked for advice.

After Royce left last night she had had a long chat with them about the kind, gregarious American who'd swept into her life and turned it upside down. It surprised and comforted her to sense their approval.

'Can you believe I'm going with Mollie to Holly Jolly Christmas Land today?'

'Aunty Rach, why are you talking to yourself?' Mollie stood on the kitchen doorstep. The puzzled expression filling her blue eyes was all Harry, and the resemblance twisted Rachel's heart in a tight knot.

'There's a lady at the front door. I didn't let her in because she's a stranger and we don't ever let strangers in the house.'

'Does this lady have a name?'

'I think she said it's Amy. She's wearing a uniform like my daddy.'

Oh no! Rachel's heart thumped wildly. Surely she'd have rung first if it was good news? Had the search party been too late to save her brother? While all the worst scenarios raced through her head she calmly told Mollie to go upstairs and get dressed.

Rachel forced on a smile before walking back in the house. Was the fact she could only make out one shadow through the frosted glass door a good sign?

'Good morning, Ms Trewarren.'

'Is it?'

The young woman's expression softened.

'Yes, it is. I considered phoning but wanted to tell you the news myself. We've already given the hospital an update but asked them not to say anything to Mrs Trewarren until you have the chance to speak to her.'

Tears ran unchecked down Rachel's face as she struggled to register each and every one of Amy's words. Harry was safe and his injuries were minor.

'Why don't we go inside? I'll put the kettle on.'

You funny Brits and your tea, Royce would say. He loved to joke about what he labelled their national obsession. As if by magic he stepped out of his front door and Rachel ignored Amy's disapproving frown to beckon him over. Right now she needed a hug from a giant, fluffy snowman more than anything.

The tear tracks running down Rachel's face meant one of two things but as soon as Royce held her in his arms and stared into her glittering eyes he knew for certain.

'Harry is safe.'

'Yes, isn't it wonderful?' Her breath

hitched and a brilliant smile lit her face.

'Did I miss something again?' Mollie glared at them all.

'Oh dear, the press have started to arrive. I was afraid it wouldn't take long to leak out.' Amy Worthing glanced back towards the road.

'Let's all get inside unless you want to be plastered over the front pages of the tabloids. They love a heart-wrenching Christmas story with a happy ending.'

Royce steered the officer into the house and slammed the door behind them.

'Is my daddy all right?' Mollie's voice wobbled and her face turned as white as Royce's snowman jumper.

Royce swept the little girl up in his arms.

'Sweetheart, he's back safely at his base and fine. I promise.'

'Is he sick?'

'Only a little bit,' Captain Worthing chimed in. 'He's got to see the doctor today and then we'll find out when he can come home.'

'But I need him right now!' Mollie

wailed. She buried her face in Royce's neck and her hot tears stuck to his skin. He understood there were army procedures to go through including debriefings and medical checks but this sweet girl who simply missed her father couldn't understand that.

'I know you do.' Rachel threw him a helpless glance.

'Hey, kiddo, do you remember what's on your Christmas wish list for today?'

'We're going to make presents this morning and see Father Christmas and pet a reindeer at Holly Jolly Christmas Land this afternoon.' Her face brightened as she rattled off their plans.

'If you like, we could sneak over to my house now and get busy on the gifts. I think Aunty Rach has a few secret things to do here.'

'What secret things?'

'They won't be a secret if I tell you.' Royce winked. 'Never ask too many questions before Christmas.' He tapped the side of his nose.

Judging by the growing number of

press vehicles outside Rachel would have a problem again getting out of the house. He'd rely on Captain Worthing to solve that particular problem. He'd concentrate on taking Mollie's mind off when her father might make it home.

'I can't get my shoes and a coat unless you put me down.' Mollie's bossy streak popped back out and he quickly did as he was told. 'I want to make something extra special for Daddy.' She raced off upstairs.

'Thank you, Mr Carver. That simplifies things tremendously.' Amy nodded at Rachel. 'Let's go.'

'But what about . . .'

The officer's eyes twinkled.

'An army staff car is waiting for us at the end of the lane running behind these houses. One hop over the fence and we'll be good.'

'Don't fret.' Royce gave Rachel a swift kiss. 'Everything's under control here. You go give Anna the good news.' Shooing them off he prepared for a morning of glitter, cotton-wool balls and glue.

★ ★ ★

'Really? You're absolutely sure Harry's all right?' Anna gripped Rachel's shoulders and tears seeped from her weary eyes.

'I promise. I'll get Amy in and she'll tell you the details.'

On the way to the hospital the liaison officer let Rachel in on something they had planned. Anna wouldn't be the only one in tears if they pulled this off.

Rachel stuck her head around the door and beckoned to Amy.

'Good morning, Anna. Isn't it lovely news?' Amy set up her laptop on the bed tray. 'I've got some maps and photos of the area to show you where Harry was found.'

'Oh, right.'

Rachel stifled a smile. After five minutes of detailed explanations about the generous family who took in Harry and cared for his minor injuries she sensed Anna beginning to flag. The familiar beep of an incoming Skype call filled the room and out of the blue came her brother's raspy, deep voice.

'Harry?' Anna's initial disbelief transformed into a brilliant smile. She stroked her fingers over the screen, lingering on her husband's new bushy beard.

'Was Mollie's birth really so bad you had to get yourself ambushed to avoid being here this time around?' A tremor ran through her voice.

'I'll be home soon,' Harry promised and it broke Rachel's heart to see her brother reach out to match his hand against his wife's in a desperate effort to touch her and his unborn twins. 'Is my sweet Mollie OK?'

'She's a trooper.'

'Hug her from me.'

The connection crackled and Harry's picture started to break up before fading to a blank screen.

'I'm grateful he's alive . . . I know we're lucky . . . but I need him right now!' Anna sobbed out her frustration.

Hearing her sister-in-law echo Mollie's words finished off Rachel, too, and they clung to each other while Amy quietly disappeared from the room.

All I Want for Christmas

Royce sneaked a glimpse at his phone while Mollie carefully printed her name on the last gift tag.

'On our way from the hospital,' the text read. 'Be with you in a few minutes. I'll creep in the back way.'

'Aunty Rach will be here soon. Do you want me to hide her present here and I'll give it back to you on Christmas Eve to put under your tree?'

'No, thank you. If I put it there today she can shake it and wonder what it is.' Mollie's logic made him smile. Anticipation was half the fun of Christmas.

They'd included plenty of cotton wool balls in the manicure-in-a-jar kits they put together for Anna and Rachel so hopefully the bottles of nail varnish wouldn't break. Along with those they'd made more of the lollipop stick photo frames too. But Harry's gift was the best.

Rachel and Royce had taken photos on each of Mollie's Christmas wish days and selected the best to put in a mini scrap book. He purposely left the last few pages blank to add more pictures from their last few outings. Mollie decorated the cover with a crayon drawing of Harry almost obliterated by green glitter. Royce punched holes in the pages and threaded through red and green ribbons to hold it all together.

'Let's get this mess cleaned up and we'll eat lunch as soon as Aunty Rach arrives because . . .'

'We need to get to Holly Jolly Christmas Land!' Mollie bubbled over with excitement.

A light tap on the kitchen door sent the little girl running and she practically dragged her aunt inside, talking nineteen to the dozen.

'What did you make for your mummy?'

Mollie shook her head.

'I'm not telling you.'

Royce caught Rachel's eye and she quickly changed the subject.

'Do I smell Reindeer Rolls baking?'

'You sure do.'

'Mollie . . .'

'Go to the toilet and wash my hands. I know.' She rolled her eyes and flounced out.

'Six going on sixteen.' Rachel sighed.

'Come here.' The words barely left his mouth before his arms were full of warm, perfumed loveliness. Royce cupped the back of her head and drew her closer. 'Oh yeah. You slay me, Ms Trewarren.'

'You're not bad yourself. On the kissing scale that is.'

'Not bad? That's hardly a ringing endorsement.'

Her eyes gleamed brighter than Christmas tree lights.

'Maybe the score will improve on your second attempt.'

'Only maybe?' Royce kissed her again which wasn't exactly a hardship.

'Yippee!' Mollie barrelled back in and threw her arms around his legs. 'Can I be a bridesmaid? I've got my red dress and sparkly shoes. They're perfect.'

'Shush, Mollie for goodness' sake,' Rachel hissed. 'What did I say?'

'Not to tell Mr Roy I heard you talking about loving each other.' She beamed. 'But it's all right now because he kissed you like my daddy kisses Mummy. That means you'll get married and have babies.'

Stifling the rumble of laughter bubbling up in his chest was the hardest thing he'd ever done but if he succumbed Rachel would be even more humiliated.

'We are not getting married.' Her emphatic response stung. Did she need to sound quite so appalled?

Mollie's smile collapsed.

'Why not?'

'Because we're going to Holly Jolly Christmas Land instead,' Royce declared. 'Much more fun. Come on.' Did he imagine the sliver of disappointment filtering through Rachel's eyes? 'Didn't you tell Aunty Rach it's compulsory to wear something Christmassy?'

'She only wears boring old black.'

'I intended to change into something more . . . colourful but I didn't have time.'

'Borrow one of Mr Roy's jumpers.' Mollie grinned. 'He's got lots.'

Royce fixed Rachel with a challenging stare.

'Fine.' Her bright red face could stand in for Rudolph's nose. 'Pick the smallest one you've got and I'll wear it.'

'Deal.' Call him mean but he had the perfect jumper in mind.

* * *

Even in the sea of Christmas jollity Rachel stood out. The fluffy scarlet jumper hung down to her knees doing nothing to help her bizarre appearance.

'I kinda made this one myself,' he'd told her. 'Took a regular sweater and used Velcro to stick everything on to make it easier to wash.'

White sparkly tinsel decorated the neck, wrists and hem. A big green felt tree dominated the front, hung with all the gifts from the twelve days of Christmas song including fake pears and a moulting partridge. Miniature lights.

The words over-the-top didn't come close to describing the monstrosity he'd gleefully decked her out in.

This was her penance. Rachel wasn't stupid. When she mocked Mollie's marriage suggestion he cut back with a careless reference to the Christmas theme park being far more fun while his smile faded away.

If she tried to explain that the general idea of marriage scared her rather than marriage to him in particular, Royce would demand she be more specific. Rachel couldn't bear to admit she was a coward.

After she watched her father lose the will to live when he lost her mother, the core of her fear rested in the sheer vulnerability of loving someone that deeply. So why did she say those three dangerous words to Royce the other day?

Royce crouched down beside a dark-haired little boy and pointed various things out in the park while he rested a reassuring hand on the child's shoulder. Slowly a tentative smile replaced the boy's wide-eyed fear.

That's why you love him, she told herself.

'Is everyone ready to see Father Christmas?' Mark Tremayne, the group leader, clapped his hands.

When they had arrived and parked next to the two mini-buses from the children's support group Mollie immediately struck up a friendship with a quiet red-haired girl about the same age. Elsa's parents died a couple of years ago and she lived with her grandparents in Newquay who struggled to take care of her.

'What are you going to wish for, Aunty Rach?'

This jumper to disappear? She caught Royce's satisfied grin.

'I'm not sure. How about you? Do you want more furniture for your doll's-house?' Rachel purposely didn't suggest ice skates because in about another six weeks the rink would close until next winter. She hated that there wasn't a year-round rink in the area these days.

'Not really. I just want Mummy, Daddy and the twins home for Christmas.'

How on earth could she explain that probably wouldn't happen? Even if the babies were born today Anna probably wouldn't be able to bring them home that soon and they'd no idea when Harry would make it back from Afghanistan. In her last update Amy was doubtful he'd be cleared by the army and transported home for at least another week.

'I'm sure Father Christmas will see what he can do.' Royce patted her head.

'You shouldn't promise . . .'

'I didn't.' He smiled at Mollie. 'You know he doesn't promise children gifts but he does his best.'

'I know, Mr Roy.' Her niece's solemn nod tugged at Rachel's heart. For a six-year-old she often understood too much.

The two little girls raced ahead to catch up with the group and Royce grasped hold of Rachel's hand.

'She needs hope. We all do.' His eyes darkened. 'Don't we, honey?'

'I suppose.'

'I know what I'm gonna ask for.'

Rachel couldn't speak.

'I could use a new Frosty the Snowman jumper. Mine's a bit bedraggled.' He gave her a searching look. 'That's not the whole truth but it'll do with little ears around.'

Her neck flamed to match her jumper.

'You coping OK with coming back here?'

'It's smaller and noisier than I remember.'

'You're bigger and quieter.'

'I suppose.' She shrugged. 'It's wonderful to see Mollie so happy.'

A Baffling Transformation

Thanks to the overnight drop in temperature, icy rain blew straight across the railway tracks to sting Royce's face like vicious pinpricks. He stamped up and down the platform waiting for his mother's train to arrive and prayed it wouldn't be late or she'd be met by an icicle.

There'd been a strained silence after he passed on his father's message before Marilyn insisted hell would freeze over before she spoke to Stuart Carver again. Strangely he felt the harsh retort popped out automatically rather than coming from the heart.

The train rumbled in and he scanned the platform for his mother among the few passengers getting off. It surprised him to spot her dressed in a bright red rain slicker and matching rain hat instead of her usual unobtrusive dark colours.

'Merry Christmas!'

His mother's jovial greeting shocked him and then she enveloped him in a tight hug, completely knocking him for six. A good day normally included a handshake if he was lucky.

'How was the journey?'

'Excellent.'

'It's a long way to come on your own.'

'That was the best thing about it.' The sharp response made him smile. 'I didn't have your father fussing and complaining. On the plane I sat next to an interesting man from Egypt and we ended up swapping e-mail addresses to keep in touch.'

'Really?' Royce wasn't sure which amazed him most, the fact his shy mother chatted to a stranger or that she had an e-mail address. His father always claimed she wasn't smart enough to understand computers and forbade her to touch his laptop.

'Yes, really. Do you mind if we get out of this rain? I want to hear all about this Rachel person.'

After his chat with Rachel last night he wasn't sure how to reply. Mollie didn't argue when Rachel suggested she go straight to bed after their hot chocolate.

'You want to know what I asked Santa for?' He'd sneaked the question in before she could avoid the subject again. 'I asked for a chance with you.'

'And I'm not giving you one now?'

'Some days yes, others are a definite no.'

He tried to be straight with Rachel but she didn't return the favour and they left things flying higher up in the air than a helium balloon.

An idea niggled in his brain but he'd need help from Rachel's old ice-skating coach to pull it off. Royce wasn't a man for conventional romantic gestures but the sort of woman who enjoyed those things rarely interested him and he was 99 percent sure Rachel wouldn't be won over by a bunch of red roses.

'Royce, my feet are two blocks of ice. How about you come out of dreamland and open the car?'

'Sorry.' His sheepish apology made her laugh and they headed off in a good mood. Who knew if it would last?

Rachel frowned at her reflection in Anna's bedroom mirror. Most women wouldn't consider a red and black houndstooth wool tunic, slim-fitting red trousers and black leather ankle boots radical Christmas fashion choices but for someone who rarely deviated from wearing all black? It ranked up there with streaking naked down the high street.

When her sister-in-law wasn't imitating a beached whale they wore similar sized clothes so she'd raided Anna's wardrobe for their pantomime excursion.

'Cool, Aunty Rach.' Mollie skipped in. 'Mummy always wears the troll earrings I gave her with that jumper.'

Trolls? What were they to do with Christmas?

'I can't wear your mum's . . .'

'You have to. Mr Roy will love them.' Her niece ignored Rachel's protest and rifled through Anna's top dresser drawer. 'Here.'

With their tufts of bright red hair

and Father Christmas costumes the dangling troll earrings resembled the pencil toppers Rachel had as a child. She dutifully removed her elegant gold hoops and replaced them with the ugly earrings. Mollie was right about one thing — Royce would love them.

Her phone buzzed with a text message.

'My mom's coming with us. Thought you'd appreciate a heads-up.'

What a wonderful first impression she'd make decked out like this.

'Come on, Mollie. Let's go.' Another Christmas memory briefly knocked her sideways. Before their last family visit to Holly Jolly Christmas Land they went to see 'Sleeping Beauty', that year's St Mervyn pantomime.

'What's wrong, Aunty Rach?'

She couldn't speak.

'I miss my mummy and daddy but they're coming home soon so it's OK. Elsa told me at the park that her parents died and it makes her sad. Is that why you're sad, too?'

'Yes, it is.'

'I'm sorry. Do you want a hug?' Mollie flung her arms around Rachel's waist. If only she could bottle this moment to show Anna and Harry what a wonderful daughter they'd nurtured.

'Thank you. You're a sweet girl.' She blinked away tears. 'Let's go or we'll be late.'

A tall, big-boned woman dressed in red stood by Royce's car.

'I'm Marilyn and at a wild guess I'd say you're Rachel. You must be Mollie — what a cutie pie you are.'

'I've never had a . . . what you said. Does it taste like apples?' Mollie's response set Marilyn off and her peal of laughter was the mirror image of her son's good-natured humour. This was nothing like the reserved woman she'd expected from Royce's description.

★ ★ ★

Thank goodness he was viewing his first pantomime with a native Brit or he'd be

208

totally confused by now. The principal boy was played by a long-legged young woman and a huge, muscular man played the comedic dame.

Any resemblance to the original fairy tale was superficial and the script appeared to be written by someone with the typically British dry, sarcastic sense of humour mixed with a heavy touch of slapstick.

Every time the evil sheriff character appeared the audience booed and hissed and shouted warnings to the rest of the cast that the villain was 'behind you'.

'You don't have anything like this?' Rachel whispered.

'We sure don't but it's fun.' He slipped his arm around her shoulder, feeling sixteen again and on his first date with Alison Williams scared stiff that she'd slap him. Before he could sneak a kiss the lights went up.

'It's the interval. Time for ice-cream.' His mother pulled a wad of notes out of her purse and shoved them in his direction. 'Take Mollie with you and buy ice-creams for all of us.'

Royce caught Rachel's flash of panic but what could he do?

'I want a strawberry lolly.' Mollie dragged him along to join the queue of people at the front of the small theatre. He half listened to her babble while keeping an eye on the two most important women in his life, on pins and needles about how the conversation was going. When they'd bought their snacks he hurried Mollie back to their seats.

'I've told your lovely lady it's crazy for us both to fix Christmas dinner.' His mother beamed. 'We'll do it together.'

'Sounds great but I don't know what Rachel's got planned . . . She might . . .'

'They're going to visit Mollie's mom in the hospital but that's it.'

'Rachel, is this all right with you? You don't . . .'

'Of course it is.' His mother cut him off. 'This little sweetheart told me we're having hot chocolate with marshmallows when we get home.' She patted Mollie's head.

'I thought you'd want an early night after your journey.'

'Don't worry I'll be 'tired' after the hot chocolate and leave you two love-birds alone.'

Rachel's embarrassment equalled his own. Thankfully the second act started and forced an end to the awkward conversation. Rachel would string him up for this later.

Back home, after Mollie had gone to bed and Marilyn had returned next door, Rachel turned to Royce.

'Your mum's . . .'

'Nothing like I described? Baffles me, too.' Royce sounded weary. 'I knew she'd take to you right away, though.'

'Do you think there's a chance your parents might get back together?'

'Who knows?' He shrugged. 'They'd have to talk first and that doesn't look likely anytime soon. I'm sorry she railroaded you about Christmas Day.'

'Are you? Just say if you don't want us all to eat together.' Rachel bristled.

'You're tying me up in knots again.

What the heck do you want?' Exasperation poured out of him.

'Why? Are you trying to copy Father Christmas now and grant my wishes?'

Royce tossed a cushion out of the way and jumped up.

'It's been a long day and in a minute I'm gonna say something I regret.' He thrust his hands in front of him to warn her off. 'You know where I am if you want me. The ball's in your court. Even nice guys have limits.'

This wasn't how she pictured the day ending.

Amy Worthing's name flashed up on her phone.

'Yes?' A deep frown etched into Royce's face as he heard the tremor in her voice.

'Really?' Her voice wobbled and her knees threatened to give way.

Never Too Late?

'Sit down, honey.' Royce eased her into the nearest chair. He managed to pick up bits of the conversation while Rachel's pallor slowly warmed to something close to normal. She cleared her throat, thanked Amy and dropped the phone into her lap.

'Harry's on his way home!' Tears trickled down her face and mixed with a smile wide enough to span the Grand Canyon. 'Someone heard about the babies being due and rushed through all the formalities. He's on an RAF flight from Camp Bastion to Brize Norton. They'll put him on a connecting flight to Newquay airport and he should land around mid-afternoon tomorrow.'

'This deserves a kiss but . . .'

'No 'but' about it.' Rachel's eyes sparkled and she yanked him down beside her.

'Trust me.' She cupped his face between her soft, warm hands before kissing him so softly he wondered if he was dreaming.

A loud hammering on the front door made him curse under his breath.

'Seriously? One day we might be lucky enough to get more than an hour's uninterrupted time together.'

He followed her out into the hall.

'Mrs . . . I mean, Marilyn. Come in.'

'I sure am sorry to barge in but I'm so mad I could scream.' His red-faced mother pushed in past them and her wet shoes left muddy tracks over the carpet. 'When I get my hands on my traitorous sister she'll wish she kept her mouth shut. Fancy telling him where I was!'

'Who?' Royce was afraid he knew the answer but hoped she'd prove him wrong.

'Your father, of course.'

'Dad?'

'Do you need your ears washed out?' She scowled. 'He's turned up, hasn't he? Cool as a cucumber. He had the cheek to ask if I'd let him come in to talk but I told him to take a hike. Now he's sitting on your doorstep and refusing to budge unless you tell him to leave. You'd better do it right now or I'll be on the next train out of here.'

Rachel raised her eyebrows.

'Sorry but I'd better go and sort this out,' Royce apologised.

'I'd offer to help but I can't leave Mollie.'

Lucky you, Royce thought.

'I'll see you in the morning.' He grabbed his mother's elbow. 'Come on, let's go see what Dad wants.'

'I know full well what he wants but . . .'

'I'm not gonna argue outside in this weather.' Royce steered her towards the door and they trailed around the path to his house.

'Hi, son.' His father struggled to get up. 'I'm . . .'

'Come in and get dried off. Then we'll talk.'

'You can do what you want. I'm not talking to him.' Marilyn barged past. 'I'm going to bed.'

'Quite a woman, isn't she?' Stuart

shook his head. 'Took me forty years to realise it and I'm guessing it's too late.'

'Perhaps not.' Royce wasn't sure why he attempted to insert a touch of hope. Because it was Christmas? 'Come on, let's get you dried off.'

★ ★ ★

Rachel tugged a baggy red jumper belonging to Anna over her nightdress, smiling at Royce's influence. Her sister-in-law almost bubbled over when they spoke last night but so far the excitement hadn't propelled her into labour.

Rachel took her mug of tea out into the garden to watch the sun rise. It took every ounce of willpower not to wake Mollie up last night to share the good news but having to wait for Harry's arrival would seem endless to the little girl. Thank goodness her niece was sleeping later than usual this morning.

'Any more tea in the pot?' Royce shouted across the fence.

'What an idiotic question.'

'Do you want company?' The note of hesitation creeping into his smooth drawl bothered her. Was he unsure of her . . . or them?

'Of course.'

He came over the wooden fence and checked out her jumper with a huge grin. 'You need a Santa face or a few jingle bells but we'll get you there. It's a start.'

'You're ridiculous. I'll fetch your tea or we can sit inside if you want.'

'Nah, I'm good. Forget the tea. It's not raining and no-one's around. Make the most of it.'

'To do what?'

'Interesting. Are we being a flirt this morning, Ms Trewarren?' He whisked the mug from her hands and set it on the wood bench.

'Me?' Rachel pretended to be offended until Royce hugged her again. 'How's the un-civil war between your parents going?'

'Talk about spoiling the moment.'

Frustration tinged his voice.

'My dad's sorry for a whole lot of stuff but I don't know it'll be enough. I'm having a hard time getting my head around his change of heart but Mom's really struggling. We ate breakfast early because nobody had slept much. She did ask Dad to pass the sugar once. That's progress, I guess.'

'Sometimes we've got to make the most of what we're offered,' Rachel suggested.

'Are you saying . . .'

'Yes.' Her unhesitating reply made him smile. 'I've decided I'm fed up living a timid life.'

'Amen. Take it from me — it's liberating.'

'Does the timing have to be right?' she mused. 'Or do we make our own?'

'I'm leaning in that direction these days.'

'We could start with a kiss and see what happens next.'

★　★　★

'Will you two be OK here with Mollie?' Royce's thinly veiled question made his folks wince. In other words can you be civil to each other while I take Rachel to the hospital? His father nodded first followed a touch more reluctantly by his mother.

'Don't answer the door.'

The early morning lull hadn't lasted long. Once the news of Harry's impending arrival home broke on the radio and television the press descended in force. Rachel's phone rang incessantly until they turned it off, warning the hospital and Anna to use Royce's number instead.

An hour ago he received a message from Anna telling them she was in the early stages of labour and needed Rachel with her.

When she'd broached the subject before, Rachel had brushed it off and assured her Harry would return in plenty of time. She wasn't sure she could cope.

'We're here.' Mollie raced in through the back door. 'Hello, Mr Roy's mum.' She peered at his father. 'Are you Mr

Roy's dad? I've got a new Christmas Candy Cane game. Do you know how to play?'

'Um, no . . . but I expect you can teach me. You're obviously a smart girl.'

Mollie dragged a red-striped box out of Rachel's overflowing tote bag.

'We need to sit at the table. You go there.' She pointed him to the side nearest the window and promptly ordered his mom to sit across from her estranged husband.

A new brand of marriage counselling?

'Are you ready to go?' Rachel's voice held a slight wobble as she turned to Royce.

'I sure am. Let's get these babies born.'

'Make sure you tell me first when Noel and Holly come out of Mummy's tummy,' Mollie ordered.

'We will.' He grasped Rachel's hand. 'I parked my car around the corner. I thought about calling a taxi but this way I can nip off to pick up Harry.'

'You're smart.'

'So are you.' Royce nodded towards

the little girl, engrossed in explaining her version of the rules to his confused parents. 'Must run in the family.'

They did the whole drive to Truro in silence and inched through the heavy traffic to make it to the maternity wing.

'Run on in and I'll go park.' Royce kissed her cold cheek. 'You're gonna ace this.'

'I'm afraid of letting Anna down and fainting or something stupid.'

'She's only asking you to do your best.'

'You're good for me,' Rachel whispered.

'I've been trying to tell you that for weeks.'

'I think I finally believe you.'

Royce shooed her out of the car and watched Rachel brace herself before striding towards the front door.

'Oi, get a move on.' The driver behind sat on his horn. 'Hurry up, mate, other people are having babies, too, you know.'

Very Special Arrival

When she made a casual remark to Anna that the length of time labour took reminded her of the one time she ran a marathon, her sister-in-law grimaced with the sweeping pain of another contraction.

'I bet you didn't run with agonising backache, nausea and two footballers fighting to get out of your stomach,' Anna pointed out.

Jekyll and Hyde had nothing on a woman during childbirth. One word out of place and the usually quiet, calm Anna became a woman possessed.

'We'll administer the epidural now.' The doctor gave Rachel a sympathetic smile. 'If you want to take a break it'll be about half an hour before we're through and Anna begins to feel some relief.'

Anna glanced at the clock.

'He won't make it in time, will he?'

When Rachel received Harry's message that his plane was delayed leaving

Brize Norton she almost wept.

'I don't know,' Rachel replied honestly. She wouldn't lie. Her sweet man drove to Newquay airport an hour ago saying it made more sense to wait there. Of course she couldn't argue with his logic but knowing he was in the waiting room had bolstered her courage. 'I'll stay if you'd rather.'

Tears welled in Anna's eyes and she dug her nails into Rachel's soft palm.

'Please. I'm scared on my own.'

They'd always got on well enough before now but with Rachel's infrequent visits and the difference in their circumstances neither would have termed their relationship as close. The last few weeks changed that and going through this together today would cement it as unbreakable.

'I'll move out of the way while the doctor gets you fixed up but we can keep talking.' She stood over to one side and encouraged Anna to talk about Harry. The couple took a huge leap of faith when her hard-charging brother proposed only six weeks after meeting Anna at a friend's wedding.

He convinced her to marry him before he left the following month on his posting to Germany and by Christmas Anna was living in a strange country, with her new husband away on military exercises and a baby on the way.

Anyone who coped with that could do anything in Rachel's opinion.

'Ah, that's better.' Anna flopped back against the pillows and the first smile in hours brightened her tired features. 'I promise not to bite your head off if you sit by me again.'

'All I'll have to do is threaten to leave and you'll behave.'

'You're awful. I've no idea why that lovely man adores you.'

Rachel's cheeks burned.

'He's such a dear, sweet man. I knew you two would hit it off.'

'Why?' On the surface Rachel couldn't see why anyone would match her up with Royce.

'You can be prickly but only because

you're afraid to let people see your softer side.' Anna patted her hand. 'No-one helped you through the grief of losing your parents and it's left its mark.' Her voice broke.

'Harry wouldn't be the amazing man he is today without your loving care.'

Rachel slid a sideways glance at the nurse updating her records and obviously trying not to intrude on their conversation.

'That's enough embarrassing you for now. We'll talk again.'

Usually she resented happily married friends interfering with her private life but today Rachel saw it from a different perspective. They wanted her to enjoy what they shared which was a generous thing, not dreadful at all.

A message popped into her phone.

'Wonderful news, Anna, they're on the way. Assuming there's no hold ups they'll be here in half an hour or so.'

'Almost time to push, Anna, but unless you're superwoman and pop two babies out faster than Lewis Hamilton winning a Formula 1 race that husband of yours will see these babies arrive.' The doctor smiled.

Rachel squeezed Anna's hand.

'We can do this.'

★ ★ ★

Harry was too tired and anxious for small talk so Royce left him alone and concentrated on driving. With the hospital in sight he shook his friend's arm.

'Nearly there, pal.'

'Cheers.' Harry rubbed his tired, bloodshot eyes. 'You're a good mate. For a Yank.'

'I'll ignore that seeing it's nearly Christmas.' For the second time that day he drove around to the maternity wing. 'I'll catch up with you when I've parked.' Harry leapt from the car and took off running. Talk about the reviving power of love.

After driving around half a dozen times Royce spotted someone leave the car park and nipped into their spot. He made it through the crowd of journalists and photographers hanging around outside the hospital and hurried up to the delivery suite waiting room, sending Rachel a quick message to let her know he'd arrived.

They've asked me to stay. Can't miss out on the last part now, he reckoned.

How long did these things take? Royce's knowledge of childbirth was sketchy. He tried sitting down but gave up after a few restless minutes and paced around like an expectant father.

After the last few weeks he felt a vested interest in Noel and Holly's safe arrival.

Outside, the grim wintry sky was heavy with impending rain and the sun was close to setting already. Despite it being Christmas Eve he wasn't wearing a festive jumper for the first time this month because the sight of his frosty-faced parents this morning made him select a sober navy shirt and dark jeans instead.

Rachel raced into the room, red-faced and shiny, with tears streaming down her cheeks.

'Is everything all right?'

'Oh, Royce.' She flung her arms around his neck and kissed him hard, almost knocking him off his feet. 'Thank you. Thank you.'

'What for?'

'Making me do that.'

'I didn't . . .'

'That was the most incredible experience ever. Anna's an absolute warrior and seeing Harry's face . . . it was totally brilliant!'

'Are the babies here safely?'

'Didn't I say?' A tiny frown wrinkled her brow. 'There are two of them.'

'I'm relieved to hear it.' Royce grinned. 'That is the usual number with twins.'

'Don't mock me. I don't know if I'm on my head or my heels.'

For the next few minutes he listened to her rattle on with more details about the delivery than Anna might be happy to have shared.

'Because they're a few weeks early the hospital wants to keep the babies in for a couple of days and obviously Anna will stay with them.'

'What about Mollie?'

'Harry will come with us and bring her back for a visit before they come home for the night. Mollie needs her daddy.'

'She sure does.'

'They've already moved Anna and the babies into a private room to keep the press at bay. Captain Worthing will make a brief statement and ask for the family to be left alone.'

'Yeah, we'll see how much good that does,' Royce scoffed.

'I know we've been annoyed by the press attention but there's so much unhappiness in the world and this could've been another of the grim stories we hear every day if things had turned out differently.' Rachel's soft smile melted him.

'I could happily dance on the roof and shout out the good news.' She gave him a searching look. 'Where's your Christmas spirit gone?' Before he could answer she clapped a hand over her mouth.

'I'm sorry. You've got every right to take a day off. I almost forgot why I came out here.'

'To tell me the babies had arrived?'

'Well, yes, but Anna and Harry want you to come and see the little sweethearts.'

'Me? Won't Mollie . . .'

'She won't know.' Rachel tugged at his hand. 'Prepare to fall in love.'

'I already have.'

'With the babies,' she whispered.

'Of course.'

★ ★ ★

Why was the sight of a man's large hands cradling a tiny baby always so affecting? Rachel couldn't drag her gaze away. Royce held Holly, wrapped in a soft pink blanket, as though she were made of glass. He'd had a turn with Noel but balked when Harry jokingly offered to tuck Holly into his other arm.

Anyone would think her brother had suggested juggling two unexploded

230

bombs. She remembered being terrified when she held one-month-old Mollie but today? Today changed everything.

After witnessing the babies emerge red-faced and screaming into the world she couldn't wait to touch them, check all their fingers and toes were there and reassure them how loved they were.

'We need Mollie here.' Anna gazed adoringly at Harry. 'And someone needs to see his big girl.'

'You should rest.' Harry brushed a kiss on her forehead. 'You've done a bang-up job.'

She rolled her eyes.

'Last of the great romantics.'

'We'll be in the waiting room, Harry, when you're ready,' Royce said. 'Come in when you've reassured your beautiful, amazing wife that she is indeed beautiful and amazing.'

'She knows.'

Rachel fought back tears as Anna and Harry linked hands and a powerful rush of envy swept through her. Meeting Royce's thoughtful gaze she discovered her overwhelming emotions mirrored in his green eyes.

'Thanks, Rachel, for everything,' Anna murmured.

'Thank you.'

'I'd better take Holly back before you get too attached,' Harry joked and retrieved his new daughter.

'Come on, babe.' Royce rested his comforting hand around her shoulder and she made it outside the door before dissolving into loud, gulping sobs.

'What on earth's wrong with me?'

'Don't you mean us? I'm not much better.' He struggled to smile. 'We're a sad pair.'

'No, we're human,' Rachel conceded, 'and it's nearly Christmas.'

'Yeah, Christmas.'

'Are you OK?'

'I will be.' Royce folded her into his arms. 'Better already,' he whispered. 'You want more out of life, too, don't you? Father Christmas will do his best to make sure you get your wish.'

'Behave yourselves, you pair.' Harry

emerged from the delivery suite, grinning from ear to ear. 'Too much of that nonsense and you'll end up here, too.'

Rachel could've killed her tactless brother until she caught Royce wink.

Worth Waiting For

He snagged a chair in the corner of Anna's hospital room and snuggled Rachel on his knee. What an extraordinary Christmas this turned out to be. Whatever he'd expected when he came to Cornwall, it certainly wasn't this.

By now he should have a portfolio of writing complete, ready to apply for his degree course but apart from a few scribblings he'd done nothing. He thought he'd spend a fairly solitary holiday, apart from attending the village activities and helping with the children's support group, but look at him now.

'Look, Aunty Rach, it's the kitchen set I wanted for my doll's-house.' Mollie's eyes shone.

Christmas was about this — not tangible gifts but the abundant sense of love filling the room. The two tiny dark-haired babies slept in their plastic bassinets wearing red onesies and soft knitted hats with their names on, oblivious to all the excitement.

Every now and then Royce saw Harry glance around at his family with awe. His friend had come within a hair's breadth of losing everything and Harry's relief must be tempered by knowing not every one of his colleagues was as fortunate.

Royce had left his parents clearing up after a successful Christmas lunch. It amazed him to see them cooking the meal together and his father taking instructions from his estranged wife without complaint. That was a first.

'I'm so happy I could burst.' Mollie's red dress fluttered in the air as she spun around the room and her shoes sparkled under the bright lights.

'I know the feeling,' Rachel murmured.

'Yeah, me, too.' Royce kissed her cheek. 'You've got to wait until early tomorrow morning for my present.'

'Why?'

'Because I said so.' She had given him a beautifully illustrated first edition of his favourite Cornish myths and legends book and upped his Christmas jumper game with an outrageous green satin three-piece suit dotted with red velvet Santa hats and fake snow.

For the final touch she tracked down a red and white candy cane striped shirt and a spinning, flashing silver bow tie.

'It'll be worth waiting for.'

Harry gathered Mollie in his arms.

'We need to let Mummy and the babies rest. We'll come back in the morning.'

'I don't want to go. It's not fair.'

Happiness could be overwhelming.

'I'm pretty sure it's hot chocolate time,' Royce suggested. 'On Christmas Day there's no limit on marshmallows.'

'None?'

'None. Aunty Rach and Daddy can have as many as they want, too.'

'OK. I suppose.'

They all struggled not to laugh and gathered up all the gifts ready to leave Anna in peace. On the way to the car Royce's suit attracted a lot of attention, especially when he grabbed Mollie's hand and sang 'We Wish You a Merry Christmas' as they danced along the pavement. Within an hour he guessed Harry and his over-excited daughter would be fast asleep.

★ ★ ★

Whatever sort of Christmas present required venturing out in the cold, dark drizzle early on Boxing Day morning before anyone else was awake? Rachel followed Royce's instructions and dressed in warm, comfortable clothes while grumbling at the inconvenience of leaving her toasty bed.

'Hi, gorgeous. You ready?'

Outside the front door stood the man in question, resplendent in her favourite snowman jumper with its grinning face flashing in the dark.

'It depends what for?'

'You'll find out. Don't ask Santa too many questions.' Royce wagged his finger.

She imitated Mollie and pretended to grumble but he ignored her.

'The car's warmed up so don't complain I'm freezing you to death although . . .' He turned away to fasten his seat belt.

'Although what?'

'Nothing.'

Liar. Rachel wouldn't spoil his surprise by pressing too hard. It shouldn't have startled her when he headed towards St Austell and turned on the road leading to the Eden Project. This man resembled an elephant and never let anything go.

'You OK with this?' Royce pulled into a parking space and rested his hands on the steering wheel.

'If you'd warned me I could have brought my own skates.'

'No problem.' He reached across the back seat to retrieve a black sports bag. 'Everything should be there.'

When she unzipped the bag her red skates peeked out and she stroked the soft leather. Rachel didn't bother to ask if the rink would be open because for an ostensibly easy-going man he never left anything to chance.

'Ready?'

'Oh, yes.' She gave his snowman's orange felt carrot nose a tug. 'Come on, Frosty.'

They linked arms and headed over to the skating rink while chatting about the babies and Mollie's excitement at being a big sister. A sick feeling swept through her. When Harry's family didn't need her any more there'd be no excuse to stay in Cornwall.

'They're not gonna kick you out, you know, and I've got three months left on my travel visa. That's a decent amount of time.'

For what?

'Talk about it later. You might . . .' There was the same hesitation again. Did Royce have more hidden up his fuzzy white sleeve than a skating session? 'Ah, there's Paddy.'

'Happy Christmas!'

Her old coach swept Rachel into a giant bear hug and his familiar aroma of strong mints and cigars knocked Rachel back to the year she turned twelve and won her first south-west junior championship.

'You've got yourself a good man.'

She didn't disagree and Royce's shy smile touched her.

'The rink's all yours.' The huge arena was decorated for the holidays with twinkling fairy lights and white illuminated snowflakes hung from the high tented ceiling.

Rachel gazed longingly at the pristine ice.

'You don't mind if I . . .'

'Mind?' Royce chuckled. 'It's the main reason we're here.'

Not the only reason? For now she'd simply enjoy his marvellous gift. The two men leaned on the barrier to chat while she headed to the dressing area. She threw her coat and scarf on one of the empty benches and sat down to put on her skates, wiggling her feet and ankles to ensure she laced them to the right degree of tightness.

Rachel walked up and down the rubber carpet bending and stretching into her old warming up exercises before taking a deep breath and gliding on to the ice.

She made a few cautious laps before trying out different turns and spins. Out of the blue Beethoven's 'Moonlight Sonata' echoed around the arena and Paddy gave her a thumbs-up sign. Her last competition piece.

With the slow build-up of the music she slipped into an almost hypnotic rhythm, the only other sound came from her skates cutting into the ice and her heart thudding against her chest. Halfway through the routine she backed off from trying a triple axel because her lack of practice and decreased flexibility would put her in severe danger of injury.

Rachel picked up speed along with the music, relishing the cool breeze in her face. Close to the end she nailed a couple of double axels and ended with Paddy's favourite Sit Spin. Her quads and lower back burned in the deep squat and she probably wouldn't be able to move tomorrow.

While she rested with her hands on the ice and gasped for breath Rachel glanced up to see Royce skating slowly around the edge of the rink before heading towards her, his face a mask of intense concentration. She stood and held out her hands to steady him.

'You said you couldn't skate without falling down.'

'Thank Paddy.'

'Why?'

His cheeks flushed.

'He gave me a couple of private lessons. I wanted to understand why you love skating so much and also be able to limp along next to you.'

'But your injured leg . . .'

'Is strong enough for this.' He flashed a grin. 'I'm not attempting any of your clever tricks and we're definitely not entering a pairs' figure skating competition any time soon.' A touch of wariness sneaked into his shy smile. 'Paddy's got a question to ask you.'

'Which I assume you know all about?'

Royce wouldn't lie. He'd bent the

truth several times today already. Paddy floated his crazy idea one day last week and each time they met, the Irishman worked on him a bit more.

'Yeah, I do. Hear him out. Please.' He lowered his mouth to kiss Rachel while praying he'd keep his balance. 'For me. For yourself . . . for us.'

'Us?'

Rachel would never be an easy woman to convince about anything but 'easy' never attracted him.

'Let's take off these instruments of torture first.' He gestured to his uncomfortable skates. 'We'll find somewhere to sit down and chat. I brought hot chocolate and leftover Christmas cookies.'

'You never give up, do you?'

'Nah, so you might as well get used to it.'

'Fine, let's hear what Paddy's got to say.'

Ten minutes later she exploded with laughter and stared at them both as though they were out of their tiny minds.

'Go into business together? The three

of us?'

He understood her bewilderment because he had reacted pretty much the same way when the older man had first spun his story.

'Think of all the kids like Rachel who never reach the stars because they don't have access to a year-round skating rink,' Paddy had said.

'We could open one here in Cornwall. I'd be the general manager but we'll hire someone for the day to day running of the facility. Rachel would be in charge of the skating programme and I think you'd do a good job with the publicity and special events.'

'But you're a dentist!' Rachel pointed out.

'I was a dentist.'

'I thought you wanted to write full time.'

'I'm sure one day I will but for now I've decided to keep it as a hobby and see what happens. I'm pretty sure I'd have a ball with this.' He squeezed her hands. 'Would you enjoy coaching young skaters or not? Yes or no?'

'Yes, but . . .'

'That's all we need for now, love,' Paddy reassured her.

'But I'm frightfully out of shape and way out of touch with skating trends.'

'Don't be worrying yourself.' He patted her shoulder. 'This won't come together overnight. There's a financial plan to put together and a suitable site to find.'

Rachel gazed at him.

'I'd better be careful what I ask Father Christmas for another year.'

'Ah, but this was one of Mollie's wishes.'

'Mollie?'

'Yeah, she whispered to me that apart from her folks and the babies being back home together she had one other extra-special wish. Mollie said she loves us, we love each other and she wants us all here together.' Royce cracked a wry smile.

'It totally made sense to me and then Paddy came up with his scheme. I reckon it all fits together pretty neatly.'

He opened up the bag and pulled out a Thermos along with three Christmas mugs.

'It's not champagne but I reckon hot chocolate is more suitable anyways in our case.'

Still bemused, she watched him pour the hot drinks and took the snowman mug he passed her. 'Here's to Christmas and the great Cornish ice project.'

'Anyone would think we're going into the ice-cream business,' Rachel joked.

'Hey, that's a great idea for the summer. We could . . .'

She plastered a firm kiss on his mouth to shut him up. Royce Carter had already worked his magic on her family's Christmas lists. He didn't need any more bright ideas.

*Other titles in the
Linford Romance Library:*

UPSATIRS, DOWNSTAIRS

Alice Elliott

Rumours are flying around the servants' quarters at Brackenfold Hall. Items are going missing, and nobody knows who to trust anymore. Fingers start pointing at Bess, the sullen new scullery maid — but housemaid Sally Halfpenny feels sure she isn't to blame. Sally vows to uncover the true identity of the thief. Meanwhile, a fever has hit the whole village, and she fears for the safety of her parents. Not to mention the anguish of her unrequited love for footman James Armstrong . . .

WHEN A WOMAN LOVES

Denise Robins

Sandra was the kind of girl men found irresistible. Hugh Lancaster, the famous artist for whom she posed, deserted his wife and was driven to suicide. Michael Hunt, the only man she ever loved, married her — but risked ruining both their lives because of her past. Then there was Victor Bentley, the debauched playboy, whose designs on her threatened to deepen the tragedy . . .

A DEBT FOR ROSALIE

Anne Stenhouse

Rosalie Garden arrives at Maldington House, an upmarket guest house, to work as a chef and earn enough to repay her father who bailed her out after her ex brought down her catering business. David Logie is the house's owner, and son of the proprietor Agnes. Still mourning the early death of his wife, David wants to sell his inheritance. Together with Agnes, Rosalie works hard to frustrate David's plans — and bring him to realise that he can love again . . .